"I depend on y[...]"

"Not true," Ben said. "I depend on you, too, you know."

"But I don't want to depend on you…on anybody. And you need to focus on Hope. We all need to get our lives back on track."

Ben studied Alyssa as if he might try to change her mind. Instead, he reached out and moved a stray lock of hair off her cheek. "I'll put dinner on the table while you pack, and I'll carry the heavier stuff over to the cottage while you put the boys down. Thanks for being so understanding with Hope. With both of us."

"The irony is that neither of you would need understanding if not for me."

"Then good thing you're worth it."

"Are you sure about that?"

"More sure than I've been about anybody in a very long time."

She bit her lip to keep from bursting into tears. How had everything gotten so complicated?

Books by Carol Voss

Love Inspired

Love of a Lifetime
Instant Daddy
Daddy Next Door

CAROL VOSS

Always an avid reader with a vivid imagination, Carol grew up in Smalltown, Wisconsin, with church ice-cream socials, Fourth of July parades, summer carnivals and people knowing and caring about everybody else. What better backdrop for heroes and heroines to fall in love?

In the years between business college and a liberal arts degree, Carol worked in a variety of businesses, married, raised two sons and a daughter and did volunteer work for church, school, Scouts, 4-H and hospice. She is an award-winning author of family stories.

Carol lives near Madison, Wisconsin, with her creative husband, her sweet, vibrating border collie and her supervisory cat. Besides writing, she loves reading, walking her dog, biking, flower gardening, traveling and, most of all, God, home and family. She loves to hear from readers at carol@carolvoss.com.

Daddy Next Door
Carol Voss

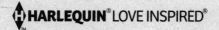

HARLEQUIN® LOVE INSPIRED®

Recycling programs
for this product may
not exist in your area.

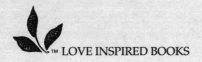

™ LOVE INSPIRED BOOKS

ISBN-13: 978-0-373-87834-5

DADDY NEXT DOOR

www.LoveInspiredBooks.com

Printed in U.S.A.

Inasmuch as ye have done it unto the least of these
my brethren, ye have done it unto me.
—*Matthew* 25:40

To couples struggling to find that balance of
sharing, loving and laughing together
that works for their family.

Chapter One

"Is everything gonna be okay, Mommy?"

Alyssa Douglas glanced from waves crashing against the shore in a rhythmic whoosh to the darkening sky to the tiny, worn cottage that was once the yellow of daffodils. Lump in her throat, she offered a smile to her worried four-year-old clutching his Braveman action figure in his little fist. "Everything will be great, Joey. We'll have a new life and so much fun you won't know what to do. I promise."

A promise she'd do everything in her power to live up to.

Joey pushed his glasses up on his nose, his squint telling her he was still worried.

It would take time, but she hoped with all her heart that their move to Rainbow Lake would help him grow into the happy four-year-old he could be.

She dragged her baby's car seat from her Escalade and tucked Robbie's blankets to shield his face from the cold wind. Grasping the carrier in one hand, she headed for the cottage, the roar of the lake filling the deepening dusk.

She hardly recognized the lake as the same one she'd befriended as a child. No doubt, it liked summers better than Novembers, too. Her fingers clumsy with anticipation, she unlocked the door and walked inside, a heavy pine scent hitting her.

Joey wrinkled his nose. "It smells funny."

"It's cleaning solution. The man who takes care of the cottage must have used it after I let him know we were coming." The living room wasn't as big as she remembered. The furniture looked more worn, the rugs older, more faded and the walls needed fresh paint.

But with the faded slipcover on the sofa reminding her Gram had let her help sew it, the same confidence settled over her that always had when she'd stayed here during summers as a child. Gram's cottage was exactly where she needed to be. On her own. Away from the generous people who'd made her and her boys their "project" this past year.

Not that she hadn't needed their help. She didn't know how she would have survived without it. And she'd always be grateful.

But she didn't need it anymore. Now, she needed to get back on her feet and learn to stand on her own without everybody, especially her parents, rushing in to help her at every turn.

She wished Gram were still here.

She blinked away the sting of tears and shut the door against the wind, effectively muffling the lake's fury. She only hoped Gram's determined, positive vibes still lived within these walls. She needed that energy and strength to get established and find a job and child care before her parents came for Christmas. She didn't know any other way to convince them to stop worrying about her and the boys.

She set her sleeping baby's car seat in the once-plush green velvet chair—the chair she'd curled up in as a kid to paint or read or daydream. Gram had encouraged daydreaming, a secret Alyssa had kept from her parents. She smiled through her tears.

Robbie didn't stir. He'd been sleeping since she'd pulled off the road and nursed him, and she needed him to keep napping until she could get Joey settled. Shivering, she tucked the blankets more snugly around her baby. Winter in the drafty cottage in northern Wisconsin was going to be a whole different thing than it had been in the comfortable colonial they'd left behind in Madison.

"Joey, come help me build a fire, okay?" She perched on the hearth and began to lay wood in the fieldstone fireplace, Gram's lessons on fire building sifting through her mind. "You can hand me the smaller pieces."

Joey dropped to his knees beside her. "Why doncha turn on the fire like at home?"

"This fireplace is different. It burns real wood." Had he understood her explanation that the house he'd always lived in would soon be somebody else's home?

"What are those for, Mommy?" He pointed.

Jamming the kindling Joey handed her under the logs, she spied two long, shaved sticks leaning against the fieldstone, a memory warming her. "Gram and I used to put marshmallows on the end of those sticks and toast them over the fire."

He studied her face. "Can we do that?"

She heard the timid plea in his voice, as if he expected her to be too busy. Her heart ached for him. She'd been too busy a lot…with her high-risk pregnancy, then the new baby and now, their move. "We can do anything we want to, and that includes toasting marshmallows. I packed a big bag in the trailer just for us."

She crumpled some of the yellowed newspapers on the hearth and stuffed them around the kindling, then struggled with the lever to open the flue. It finally gave with a rusty clank, breaking two of her fingernails in the process.

A perfectly good manicure down the drain. *It's a small thing, Lissa.* Gram had always chided her concern over things Gram identified as unimportant. A couple of broken nails certainly qualified. Alyssa took a long match from the box on the mantel and struck it against the side of the container.

Nothing. She struck it again. And again. Still nothing. She tried another match with similar results. They'd need to snuggle to stay warm if she couldn't get a fire lit.

She'd brought warm blankets for their beds, but the drafty cottage was obviously too much for the old furnace. Besides, she'd promised Joey toasted marshmallows. "Let's see if we can find better matches in the kitchen."

"'Kay." Joey jumped up and scurried at her side.

Snapping on the light switch, she walked into the white-washed beadboard room, her boots clicking on the worn linoleum. One glimpse of Gram's battered, round table set off memories of sharing homemade lemonade and chocolate chip cookies. Such treats had followed lessons on building a fire, chopping wood, fishing or catching fireflies. Memories she wouldn't trade for the whole world. She hoped she remembered enough to teach Joey how to fish and catch fireflies come spring.

"Is this the kitchen?" Joey looked around as if expecting the room to open up like their spacious one in Madison had.

"This is it." The kitchen was even smaller than she remembered. Was it big enough to expand the table for Christmas dinner? Did Gram have table leaves? She'd have to look for them.

She quickly moved to the fifties stove. Would the oven hold a turkey? Did the stove even work?

"Where are the matches, Mommy?"

"Matches?" She looked at Joey. "Right." She pulled out a drawer and felt around until she grasped the familiar tin box. "Here they are, exactly where Gram always kept them."

"Is she here?"

"Gram?" Gram was here. Alyssa could feel her. What she wouldn't give for one of her warm hugs. But no matter what she felt, she couldn't confuse Joey. "No, honey. Gram died this past spring."

"Did she go to heaven? Like Daddy?"

"Yes, she did." She waited for another question. She hoped it wasn't about heaven. Heaven was a mystery she had no idea how to explain. To him. Or to herself.

But instead of asking a question, Joey turned and zoomed into the living room. "Come on, Mommy. Let's start the fire."

Relieved there would be no questions she didn't know how to answer, at least for the moment, she followed him and knelt at the hearth. She struck a match and touched it to the newspapers inside the firebox. Holding her breath, she watched a flame flicker into being and begin to build. "Yay, we have a fire." She pulled the screen shut and stood. "I'm going to bring in some things from the car."

"I wanna go with you," Joey whined.

How long would it take before he stopped worrying she'd never come back? Like Cam. "I need you to be brave and stay by your brother. Can you do that?"

He nodded in his anxious way.

When she pulled the door open, the crash of waves vamped to full volume. She shut the door behind her, buttoned up her wool jacket and headed into the wind.

She fished her keys out of her jacket pocket, unlocked the padlock on the U-Haul trailer and climbed inside. Reaching across Joey's sled and her bike, she grabbed the grocery bags. She set them on the ground outside, then climbed back in the trailer and found blankets, Robbie's Pack 'N Play and Joey's bag of books. She'd wait until morning to unload the rest.

Leaving things stacked near the U-Haul for another trip,

she picked up the grocery bags and strode to the cottage. The smell of something burning drew her eyes to the chimney. Black smoke puffed into the night. Good. The fire was building in the fireplace. Soon, they'd be cozy and warm.

But the chimney glowed oddly orange against the darkening sky.

Something was wrong. Her boys— Dropping the groceries, she raced for the door.

Ben Cooper hung his leather jacket on a peg in his laundry/mudroom and tried to distinguish what the charred stink was that his kitchen fan couldn't keep up with. Had Hope tried to cook a recipe she'd picked up in family living class again?

He guessed he shouldn't be surprised. The tried-and-true had always been too boring for her. Maybe whatever she'd burned wouldn't taste as bad as it smelled. Holding that thought, he headed for the kitchen. "Honey, I'm home."

"How's it goin', Dad?" Hope's dark, curly head stayed bent over one of the pots on the stove. In her usual after-school attire—worn jeans with holes in the knees, one of his old gray sweatshirts that fit her like a tent and bare feet no matter the weather—she fiercely stirred whatever was burning as if she thought she could still save it. "Digger sounds excited."

"Probably checking out the car and trailer parked next door. Funny, thought, Clyde said Emma's granddaughter would arrive next week."

"Did you see anybody?"

"Nope." Trying not to let the scorched-food smell get to him, Coop thumbed through the day's mail stacked on the island counter, a return address giving him a nudge of optimism. He slipped a finger under the flap, shook the letter from its envelope and skimmed words of praise for the church Reclamation Committee's ambitious undertaking to turn an unused building into low-income housing.

Finally, he homed in on "Unfortunately, economic considerations leave us no choice but to decline your invitation to contribute. Perhaps at a future time…"

He blew out a breath. A vague promise of future support sure wouldn't pay for the lumber and fixtures they needed to make the Burkhalter Building into apartments.

Hope carried a pan around the center island, wooden spoon bouncing against the side with each step. "You'd better be hungry 'cause I made lots of beef Stroganoff."

Burned Stroganoff? He could hardly wait. He tossed the letter on the counter with the rest of the mail. Digger's barking outside was getting under his skin. "What is that dog making such a racket about? I'd better get him. Last thing we need is Mrs. Hendrickson calling Sheriff Bunker again."

He strode to open the back door and whistled.

Dig finally came panting around the corner, but instead of trotting into the house he turned and ran away, yipping excitedly and glancing back at Coop as if he expected him to follow.

"What has you so agitated, boy?" Coop reached for his jacket. "Be back in a minute."

"Does he smell like skunk?"

Noting the disgust in her voice, he shrugged into his jacket. "I think he learned his lesson about skunks."

"I hope so. I don't think we have any tomato juice to pour over him. Not that it helped much."

She was right about that. Living with a dog sprayed by a skunk was an unpleasant experience best not repeated. He pulled the door closed and strode in the direction his dog had disappeared. "Give it up, Dig. I hope you haven't rooted out a bear because if you have, we're both in big trouble."

What was that smell? It sure wasn't skunk.

It was…something burning.

He rounded the corner of his house. Smoke rode the wind and billowed from the old cottage next door. Fire flashed from the chimney. "Well, will you look at that? She set the chimney on fire."

Grabbing his cell phone from his belt, he punched 9-1-1 and took off at a dead run. Directing the dispatcher to the cottage, Coop raced past the Escalade and trailer, dodged a pile of stuff on the ground and jumped over spilled groceries. Replacing his cell, he thundered onto the porch, pounded on the door and shoved it open. A bad-smelling, dark smoky haze filled the place. "Where are you?" he yelled.

A baby's cries came from somewhere, probably the kitchen.

Adrenaline slamming him, Coop shot through the room toward the cries, the kitchen doorway appearing in the gloom.

"Don't let go of my hand, Joey," a woman's voice said urgently. "The back door is stuck or something. We have to go through the front door to get out."

"But more smoke is in there," a child whimpered.

Coop strode toward the shadowy figures taking shape, swept the kid into his arms and grasped the woman's smooth hand. "You have the baby?"

"Yes."

"Then let's go."

"I dropped Braveman!" the kid hollered, twisting to get free.

Coop gripped the boy tighter, peering through the haze for a small animal of some kind. "Who's Braveman?"

"My superhero."

"Then he should be fine, right?" Smoke stinging his eyes, he made for the door. The baby's cries echoing eerily in the haze, they broke onto the porch. Cold, fresh air smelled mighty sweet. They thumped down the few steps.

The woman set the baby carrier on the ground and fumbled with the security strap, the baby's crying almost covered by the wind.

Coop wrangled himself out of his jacket and wrapped it around the shivering kid in his arms. "You okay?"

The boy coughed, tears rolling under his glasses and down his cheeks. "Braveman's in danger," he wailed.

Coop glanced up at the black smoke rising into the sky and decided Braveman was on his own for the time being. "Don't superheroes love danger?"

The little guy gave a serious nod.

"Well, he's probably doing great, then."

The woman tried to cuddle her infant inside her jacket. "I need to call the fire department," she said over the baby's crying.

"I already called them."

"Oh. Thank you so much."

Coop helped her grasp blanket ends whipping in the wind and tucked them tightly around the infant. The woman's face was shadowed by the night, but her exotic scent drew him in and commanded his attention. With those high heels, she could almost look him in the eye. He liked that.

"I'm sorry to be so much trouble." Swaying to comfort her baby, her deep sapphire eyes fired off enough damsel-in-distress signals to tweak every protective nerve he owned. Her teeth were even chattering.

"Glad to help." This wind had ice in it, and her lightweight jacket was clearly built for style rather than warmth. "My house isn't far away."

"Your house?" The woman sounded as if she hadn't considered what she'd do beyond getting out of the smoke.

"Come on." Hanging on to the squirming kid, Coop

scooped up the empty baby carrier and strode across the yard Clyde kept mowed and trimmed. The woman caught up and jogged beside him, the baby still crying his heart out. He sure did have a great set of lungs.

"My brother is really, really scart."

"I'll bet he is." This kid was probably plenty scared himself. "But everybody's safe, so there's no reason to be scared."

"Braveman's not safe." Coughing, the kid turned himself into a squirming octopus trying to wrench himself out of Coop's arms again.

Coop hung on.

The woman looked over her shoulder. "Something is wrong with the chimney."

Her skin looked porcelain in the moonlight peeking through the clouds. "Birds, chipmunks, maybe even raccoons probably filled the chimney with nests and stashes of food. I'm surprised Clyde didn't clean it out before you arrived."

"I told him I'd be here next week, but…plans changed. How far do the firefighters have to come?"

"From Noah's Crossing, about a mile." Digger trotted to them, wagging his tail and looking pretty proud of himself. "Good boy, Digger."

"Is he your dog?" the boy asked.

"He sure is. He let me know about the smoke."

"He's a hero," the boy said, his voice hushed. "Just like Braveman."

"Hear that, Dig? You're just like Braveman."

"Thank you, Digger. And Mr.—" The woman sounded out of breath.

Remembering those high-heeled boots she wore, he slowed his pace. "Ben Cooper."

"Alyssa Douglas. It never occurred to me the chimney could be plugged."

"Well, don't worry. We have the best volunteer fire department and EMS unit in the area."

"Volunteer?" She sounded alarmed.

"Best in the area. We'd be in big trouble if we had to wait for help to come from farther away."

The baby's crying seemed to be winding down. Reaching his house, Coop pushed open the door and stood back to allow her to go in first.

She walked into his laundry room, the light making her golden hair glow like soft silk. He'd never seen a more delicate, feminine woman. Tall—too thin—but she carried herself like a princess. Her U.S. senator father must be proud.

Coop stepped into the house behind her. Princess or not, her problems obviously ran a lot deeper than a chimney fire. Why else would she be staying in an old cottage in November with two little kids and no husband in sight?

Chapter Two

Alyssa hurried into Ben Cooper's warm, bright laundry room, the smell of scorched food snagging her attention for a moment. She hugged Robbie close. He couldn't be as cold as she was, or he'd still be crying. She scrutinized her baby's flushed little face.

Fussing hoarsely, he blinked up at the recessed ceiling lights.

Was he flushed and hoarse from crying? Or was it something to worry about? His body was so tense. Rubbing his back, she peered at Joey in Ben's arms.

She reached out and removed his smudged glasses. Tears clumped her son's long lashes, and his eyes looked bloodshot, his gaze glued to the big yellow dog slurping water from a dish in the corner. He was so excited over the dog that it was hard to tell if he was okay or not.

She turned her attention to their rescuer. She'd just launched into their new life, and she already needed help? She could hardly believe it. Didn't want to believe it.

But there he stood, his shiny, jet-black hair falling almost to his collar. Wisps fell over his forehead like Joey's usually did. But that was the only thing about Ben Cooper that sug-

gested *boy*. His strong face, broad chest and biceps strain-
ing the fabric of his gray sweatshirt looked all grown-up.

Patting her baby's back to soothe him, she looked into
Ben's kind eyes, dark pools of concern mixed with male appreciation and the glint of curiosity.

She was used to male appreciation and knew how to deal
with it. And the curiosity was no surprise either. He had to
wonder what she was doing here.

"What did Dig get into this time?" A girl in tattered jeans
and faded gray sweatshirt hanging to her knees slid to a
barefoot stop in the doorway, her large brown eyes widen-
ing in surprise. "Hi."

"Hello," Alyssa said.

"Alyssa, my daughter, Hope."

Alyssa did her best to smile, not sure she pulled it off.

Ben handed Robbie's carrier to the girl, then bent and
set Joey down, his man-size jacket pooling at her son's feet.
Ben lifted the jacket off Joey's shoulders and slipped into
it, giving the boy a smile. "Make sure they have whatever
they need, Hope. I'm going to hook up water hoses and try
to keep the fire contained until the fire trucks get here."

"No." Alyssa grasped his arm. "You've done enough.
Let the fire department handle it. I don't want you taking
any chances."

He glanced at her hand on his arm, then raised his gaze,
his grin warming the room. "I don't take chances."

The kindness in his mellow voice reached through her
anxiety, almost as if they shared a connection. Ridiculous.
She'd just met the man.

"I'll send the EMS people over when they get here to
make sure everybody's okay." He turned and pushed out
the door.

"Dad will be safe. He knows about construction 'cause
he built our house." Hope's words sounded confident, but

her tone was thin with worry. Obviously, she was trying to convince herself her dad would be all right.

Alyssa felt even worse. "He promised he wouldn't take chances," she said to reassure herself as much as Hope. She stepped to the laundry tub, and rinsed Joey's smoke-smudged glasses under the faucet. Everything about the house seemed very new. "How long ago did he build your house?"

"We moved in over a year ago, but it took a long time to build before that."

"You've got a great dog." Joey stared at the big canine as if he'd discovered magic.

"Yeah. Dad found him in a ditch after a car hit him. He made a deal with the vet to get Digger back in shape, and I got to help take care of him." She swung Robbie's empty carrier back and forth as she talked. "I'm gonna be a vet-erinarian. To help animals like Dig."

Joey watched the girl as if fascinated. Whether by the girl, her story or the sparkling braces on her teeth wasn't clear.

"That's very admirable, Hope." Sounding as frazzled as she felt, Alyssa dried Joey's glasses the best she could with a corner of Robbie's blanket and handed them to Joey.

He coughed as he shoved them on.

"Do you feel all right, honey?"

He nodded brightly, but his eyes still looked bloodshot.

"Can you take off your jacket?"

Was that sirens she heard in the distance? She couldn't wait until the EMTs could check her children. Everything would be fine, she tried to tell herself. But how could things be fine when she'd put her children and Ben Cooper in danger, and Gram's cottage was on fire?

"Cute baby." Hope eyed Robbie.

"He's Robert." Joey struggled out of his jacket. "But we call him Robbie."

Alyssa waited for him to tell Hope his own name, but she wasn't surprised when he didn't. She laid her hand on his head. "This is Joey."

"Hi." Hope looked down at him. "Come on in," she turned and led the way.

Handing his jacket to Alyssa, Joey trotted after the dog.

Alyssa hung the jacket on one of the pegs near the door and followed the children into an open kitchen, the whir of a ceiling fan stirring a breeze. The profusion of utensils and spilled food on the counters screamed *inexperienced cook*.

"Can I get anybody anything?" Hope offered.

Joey turned to tug Alyssa's arm. "Can I have milk?"

She hated to ask but… "Joey would like milk, please."

"No problem." Hope whipped over to the table and handed Joey an already-filled glass. "You can drink this. Dad didn't have time to eat 'cause he went to find out why Digger was barking."

Alyssa helped Joey drink from the full glass. What was Ben doing next door? Was he all right? He had to be all right.

Robbie's breathing sounded stuffy, as if he had a cold. But he didn't have a cold. Was he having difficulty breathing? She held him more upright, hoping it would help him breathe easier. She missed Cam's strong lead in a crisis. Would Hope's mother know what to do until the EMTs got here? "Is your mother home?"

The girl narrowed her eyes, her pert mouth set in an unhappy line. "My mother is dead."

"I'm sorry." The poor girl. She wished she hadn't asked. She looked at her baby, willing the EMTs to get here. The sirens seemed to be getting closer.

"Can I see the fire trucks, Mommy?" Joey's eyes were like saucers.

Alyssa took the glass of milk from him before he could spill it in his excitement.

"Come on, we can see them from Dad's room." Hope took off, the dog on her heels.

Alyssa and Joey rounded the corner into a lived-in great room with floor-to-ceiling windows that looked out on the black lake. Red lights pulsed off the water, but the trucks and cottage were out of sight. Hope and the dog had already topped the open stairway.

The doorbell rang.

A barking yellow blur of locomotion thundered down the steps. Robbie's eyes flew wide as Alyssa dodged to stay out of the dog's way. She started for the front entrance, Joey at her side. Realizing the dog was headed for the back door, she turned and hurried through the kitchen and into the laundry room. "Sit, boy," she ventured, hoping to quell the barking.

Amazingly, the dog stopped barking and sat, looking up at her with liquid brown eyes as if waiting for her next command. "Stay." She gave him a firm look and yanked the door open. "Come in, come in. I'm so glad you're here."

A tall, fiftyish man with salt-and-pepper hair and an equally fit woman, both in navy blue EMS jackets and carrying heavy-looking bags, stepped inside along with a blast of cold wind. The man turned and closed the door behind him.

"We're Liz and Max." The woman gave Alyssa and her boys a concerned look. "Coop said you all inhaled some smoke."

"I'm worried about my children. My baby's only three months old." Hardly recognizing the strained voice as her own, Alyssa and Joey led the way into the kitchen, the dog moving with her as if waiting for his next cue.

"And who do we have here?" The woman—Liz—asked Joey as she set her bag on the floor and unzipped it.

Joey frowned at the woman.

"This is Joey," Alyssa answered for him. "He's four."

"Nice to meet you, Joey." The man—Max—pulled out a

chair from the table. "Mommy, why don't you sit down with the baby, so Liz can look him over?"

Alyssa sank into the chair and turned Robbie to face Liz.

"Can I check your breathing, Joey?" Max asked.

Joey looked to Alyssa.

"It's okay, honey."

"It will take just a couple minutes, okay?" Max said.

Joey gave him a small nod.

Liz pressed her fingers to Robbie's neck, then bent and pulled a stethoscope from her bag. "Any coughing fits? Shortness of breath? Wheezing? Anything like that?"

"He sounds stuffy, and he's very hoarse. Maybe from crying. The whole thing was pretty upsetting. I'm sure he was cold when we ran outside."

"Let me listen to your lungs."

"Mine? I'm fine," Alyssa said impatiently. "But my baby's breathing doesn't seem right. He doesn't have a cold, but don't you think he sounds stuffy?"

"A little stuffy, yes. But you sure you're fine? Your children need a well mother, you know."

"I have a headache, probably the stress."

"Let me take a listen."

Alyssa shook her head. "You don't seem to understand—"

"I want you to warm the stethoscope for the baby."

"Oh."

When Liz had listened and pronounced Alyssa fine, she turned her attention back to Robbie. "If you'll unzip his outfit?"

Alyssa hurriedly pulled down the zipper.

Liz pressed the stethoscope to Robbie's tiny chest.

Joey crowded against Alyssa.

She met EMT Max's gaze.

He gave her a smile. "Joey's as good as new."

Tears stung her eyes. "Thank you."

"You're welcome."

Robbie began to fuss, and now, Alyssa could hear a definite wheeze. Her heart sped up again.

"You can zip him back up." Liz quickly draped the stethoscope around her neck, grasped her cell from its clip on her bag and hit speed dial.

"Is it serious?" Throat closing, Alyssa fumbled with the zipper on her baby's sleeper.

"I want Dr. Delaney to meet us at his clinic to check the little guy. You can hold him on the way."

She swallowed her panic. "We need to go in the ambulance?"

"The doctor will want your baby to get a tad of oxygen as a precautionary measure."

Ben strode into the kitchen, the dog scrambling up from the hardwood floor to greet his master.

Meeting Ben's eyes, Alyssa's vision clouded with tears.

He glanced at Liz talking on her cell, then to Max, as if reading what was going on.

"We'll meet you there." Liz clicked off her cell.

"Mommy, can I ride in the amblunce with you?"

"I'm sorry, Joey," Liz answered. "It's pretty crowded—"

"You can ride in my big truck with me, buddy," Ben offered. "We'll follow them. How does that sound?"

Joey frowned uncertainly at Alyssa.

Her mind raced to think of another solution. One that wouldn't require even more help from Ben.

"Don't worry, Joey will be fine," Ben said. "And we'll bring both car seats." He scooped Joey onto his shoulders. "That way, I can give you all a ride back."

Alyssa swallowed, more defeated than she'd felt in a long while. She'd come to Rainbow Lake to stand on her own. Instead, she'd needed help from the moment she arrived. From Ben, Hope, the firemen, the EMTs. Ben had even risked his life for her, her children and her cottage, and now she needed even more aid.

But he seemed to think Robbie wouldn't have to go to the hospital. That he'd be coming back with them. She needed to hold on to that right now. "I'm sorry to ask you to do that, but I would really appreciate it."

Ben gave a nod. "You just worry about the baby. His big brother and I have the rest under control."

"Ben, is Robbie gonna live in heaven with Daddy and Gram?"

Sitting beside Joey in Dr. Delaney's silent waiting room, Coop eyed the boy, glasses perched on his nose and swinging his feet several inches above the polished, gray tile floor. The kid's dad was dead? That was why Alyssa was alone? "Don't worry, buddy. Robbie's going to be fine, and he'll still live with you and your mommy. When did your daddy go to live in heaven?"

Joey squinted behind his glasses as if thinking very hard. "Not tomorrow. Yestraday."

Confused, Coop dragged a breath. Did the poor kid wake up in the middle of the night calling for his daddy, the way Hope had cried for her mommy? Was he old enough to realize his father was never coming back?

At the moment, he looked like he carried the weight of the world on his narrow shoulders. Must have figured out his baby brother's trip in the ambulance was a serious thing. "The smoke probably bothered Robbie more than you because he's so small, but he's going to be fine."

Joey nodded, but he didn't lose his anxious look.

Coop hoped he was right about the baby. *These kids' mom seems in over her head, God. She sure doesn't need a sick kid on top of everything else she's obviously trying to deal with. What can I do to help them?*

He thumbed through the stack of magazines on a nearby table, looking for something to take a little boy's mind off serious stuff.

Ken Delaney swung into the waiting room in faded jeans and a black turtleneck, minus the lab coat he wore during regular office hours. The baby's blankets in one hand, he held the door for Alyssa with the baby in her arms.

Her beautiful sapphire eyes looked shell-shocked.

Coop climbed to his feet.

Joey jumped off his chair, ran to his mother and threw his arms around her legs.

Alyssa cupped her son's face in her fingers and gave him a wobbly smile. "The doctor says Robbie will be fine."

Throat feeling thick, Coop breathed a silent thank-you as he strode to her.

Alyssa met his eyes. "The doctor thinks all that crying helped him get rid of most of the smoke."

"Just keep him warm." Ken handed the baby's blankets to Coop, then flashed a sympathetic smile at Alyssa. "I'll probably see you and your children again if you decide to stick around. Good to see you, Coop."

"You, too."

Ken retreated to the back rooms of the clinic.

Coop helped Alyssa wrap the blankets around the baby, wishing he could do something to still her shaking hands. He scooped Joey onto his shoulders and led the way to hold the door for her and the baby.

By the time they had the kids in their car seats in the backseat of his crew cab and were headed to Rainbow Lake, he had time to focus on problems ahead. Like in what shape would they find the cottage? When he'd followed the ambulance, firefighters had been pouring water onto the roof by the boatload.

Alyssa turned from looking at her kids in their car seats. "They're already asleep. They've had a very rough day."

"So have you," he said.

"I should have known better than to light a fire in a fireplace that hasn't been used for a while."

"I doubt many people would think about that."

"Well, definitely not me. I'm sorry for being such a burden."

"You're not a burden. I'm glad to help. Do you want to use my cell to call somebody?"

"I have my own." She fumbled in her jacket pockets, then shakily pressed her fingers to her forehead. "I don't know where it is at the moment, but there's nobody to call anyway." She set her lips in a determined line, as if sheer will could get her through. "Did Hope stay home alone?"

"Digger's with her. She's insulted now if I insist somebody stay with her."

"How old is she?"

"I can hardly believe she's already twelve. She grew three inches this past year. Had her hair cut short. Even let the orthodontist fit her with braces to correct her 'rabbit teeth' as she calls them. I worry she's changing too fast for me to keep up with her. But she's terrific."

"Yes, she is." A fleeting smile briefly softened Alyssa's tense expression.

"Of course, I'm her dad. I'm supposed to think that, right? I'm sure Joey's dad felt the same way."

"Yes."

"Joey said his daddy lives in heaven."

She took a quick breath.

Coop glanced at her. She looked straight ahead, distant and withdrawn. The poor woman was obviously still grieving. "How did it happen?"

"Car crash."

Sudden, then. "How long?"

"Nearly a year."

"You had your baby after your husband died. That's rough."

"Yes," she acknowledged. Silence for a beat or two. "I worry about Joey. He misses his dad so much. But moving to Gram's cottage is our new beginning." She sniffed.

He hoped she wasn't crying. "Would it help to talk to your folks?"

"My parents? Absolutely not. They'd probably be on the next flight to rescue us. That's the last thing I need."

"Don't like being rescued?"

"I don't like being a charity case."

"We all need charity sometimes."

"Believe me, I've accepted my quota over the past year. It's time to do things for myself like my gram did. That's why I moved here."

"To Rainbow Lake? Sounds like you admired your grandmother."

"Yes. I loved being here with her. She used to insist my job was to enjoy being a kid," Alyssa said softly. "My life at home was so structured that I often felt guilty for wasting time here. But Gram shared important secrets with me."

He turned onto Rainbow Lake Road. "Secrets?"

"You know…intangible things. She always knew where the best blueberries grew. Where loons and wood ducks nested. Where to find the fattest night crawlers for bait. She helped me understand about being self-sufficient."

"Ah." He couldn't imagine her silky, white hands touching a night crawler, let alone baiting a hook with it. "Your grandmother shared some of her secrets with my daughter. When we moved here, Emma became kind of a surrogate grandmother to Hope."

"I'm glad. For Hope and for Gram. I worried about her being lonely. Gramps died when I was a baby."

"She talked about him sometimes. But everybody loved Emma. She had too many friends to be lonely. Her grandson Lucas stayed a few weeks the past couple summers, too. Good kid. Your cousin, right?"

She nodded. "My father's younger sister's son. He must be almost out of high school by now."

Obviously not a close family. "He's at West Point. Emma was very proud of him. And of you."

"Thank you for telling me that."

"You're welcome. Your grandmother was a generous woman, always helping somebody out, shared produce from her garden with the whole neighborhood. And she kept Hope and me supplied with plenty of those chewy oatmeal chocolate cookies of hers."

"She was her own woman. I want to teach my children the values she taught me." Her voice trembled. "That's why I moved to the cottage."

She sure expected a lot from that run-down little place. Anyway, the fire would undoubtedly change everything. He wasn't sure there would actually be anything to salvage.

Headlights bobbed as they hit the unavoidable potholes. The fire trucks had left. He tore his gaze from the road to glance at Alyssa peering intently through the windshield as if waiting for her first glimpse of the cottage. He sure hoped it hadn't burned to the ground.

Finally, the cabin's silhouette took shape in the darkness ahead.

"Oh." The word escaped her lips on a breath. "It looks okay."

Okay might be a stretch. But it *was* still standing. He swerved into the yard and braked to a stop.

Alyssa was out of the truck and running.

He grabbed his flashlight from the seat and wasn't far behind. The stench of smoke stinging his nostrils and eyes, he jogged up the steps and through the open door, barely avoiding slamming into her.

She stood deathly still just inside the door, a shattered, dripping cell phone in her hand.

"Yours?"

She gave him a distracted nod, her gaze following his flashlight beam, which darted from burned-off electrical wires hanging from overhead beams to the soaked, smoke-blackened couch and stuffed chair near the hearth, as if she couldn't find a focus.

His flashlight spotlighted a jagged hole in the roof around the chimney that gaped like an open mouth. Water dripped into a pool on the floor, the pluck of each drop the only sound.

He tried to think of anything to do but to put his arm around her. Being a stranger, he wasn't sure she'd welcome that anyway. Giving her a moment alone was the best he could come up with. "I'll take a look in the kitchen."

He strode across the smoke-blackened living room and into the tiny kitchen. Smoke damage, but no water. Glancing around, he bent and picked up a toy figure. Braveman stared at him, dirty but still in superhero condition, just as he'd promised Joey. Coop stuffed the toy into his pocket and walked back into the living room.

Alyssa stood exactly where he'd left her. Silent tears streamed down her delicate face.

He clenched his jaw hard. How could he just stand there? How could he pretend nothing was wrong while she fell apart just feet away? How could he not do something?

It wasn't in him.

He walked across the room and pulled her into his arms. She felt soft, tender, vulnerable. "It's not as bad as it looks."

She laid her head on his shoulder. Sobs shook her slender body. She cried as if now that she'd started, she might never stop.

Nothing got him like tears. Desperate to help her feel better, he wrapped her close. Gently stroked her hair.

It had been way too long since he'd held a woman. And this woman was delicious with eyes as blue and deep as Rainbow Lake. She was lost, alone, totally out of her element with two little kids to take care of.

"I'll never be ready for Christmas now," she blurted.

He released her and took a step back. "Christmas seems the least of your problems."

"I have to be established before my parents—" She gave her head a vigorous shake. "You wouldn't understand."

She had that right. He dug his clean handkerchief out of his back pocket and handed it to her.

Shaking her head, she took a tissue from her pocket and dabbed at her tears. "I'm sorry I'm such a pathetic wreck."

"No need to apologize." He wanted to gather her back into his arms, but he held his ground.

"I appreciate all you've done for us." She didn't quite look him in the eye. "Now, I need to transfer the boys to my car."

"Where will you go?"

"I remember a bed-and-breakfast on Rainbow Lake. Is it still here?"

"Mrs. Hendrickson closed it while she recovers from gall bladder surgery."

"Oh." Alyssa was clearly disappointed. "I guess I'll have to find a place in town, then."

Coop wished he had better news. "Motels in Noah's Crossing are closed for the season. Owners head south for the winter."

"All of them?"

"There are only two."

"Oh." She nibbled her pretty bottom lip as if at a loss to figure out what to do next.

His stomach knotted. Watching her flounder was downright painful.

"I'm sure I passed a motel about an hour back."

The determination in her voice tugged at him, made him want to reassure her. But she needed more than reassurance. She needed concrete help. And that he could provide. "We have a guest room you're welcome to use for the night."

She shook her head. "That's very kind, but I can take care of this."

"What if the motel you saw is closed? As exhausted as you look, you could even fall asleep at the wheel. Stay tonight. Your problems will look more manageable in the light of day. You can decide what to do then."

Chapter Three

Alyssa sat at the island in Ben's bright, cozy kitchen while he made the hot chocolate he'd insisted she needed. Hadn't he already done enough?

She watched him stir the milk-cocoa mixture on the stove and effortlessly retrieve a bag of marshmallows from an upper cabinet shelf. The man was tireless.

She, on the other hand, was exhausted, irritable and overwhelmed with her inability to take care of herself and her boys over the past few hours. First, the fire. An accident, of course, but she'd been at fault.

Then her meltdown with Ben paled only in light of how easily she'd given in to his invitation to spend the night in his guest room. But endangering her boys by driving who knew how far when she was drained would have been foolish when he'd offered her a safe alternative.

"One marshmallow or two?" Ben looked at her expectantly.

"One, please." To make things worse, he'd helped her haul in her sleeping boys, Robbie's Pack 'N Play, their suitcases. He'd even strung heavy electric cords together to power heaters he lugged to the cottage to prevent water pipes from freezing without waiting for her to help after she'd finished tending to Robbie. How she'd ever repay him for everything he was doing for her, she had no idea.

"Here you go." He set a steamy, frothy mug of hot chocolate on the counter in front of her, the image worthy of *Bon Appétit*.

"Thank you."

"Enjoy." With a smile, he lifted his cup as if to salute her and brought it to his lips.

She took a sip of the creamy, rich chocolate. "So delicious."

"Nothing like hot chocolate on a cold, fall evening…in the Midwest anyway."

"Mmm," she agreed. "Have you always lived in the Midwest?"

He shook his head. "My dad was in the marines, so we lived all over the world while I was growing up. My mother is Vietnamese."

"Somehow, Vietnam and hot chocolate don't seem to go together, do they?"

He smiled. "My mother put berries in it."

"Berries?" She couldn't help noticing he had the warmest smile. "Healthier than marshmallows."

"It was great."

"How did you end up at Rainbow Lake?"

He thought a moment. "Hope and I moved from Chicago seven years ago."

"City boy?"

"Surprised?"

She shook her head. "You have that city edge."

"Then I guess what they say is true." He took a drink of hot chocolate.

"You can take the boy out of the city, but not the city out of the boy? What did you do in Chicago?"

"I was a reporter for the *Trib*, pretty entrenched in my

job and very involved in finding housing for the homeless. There's a real need in this country," he said with conviction. "What about you?"

"I grew up in D.C., but I always loved summers at Rainbow Lake. Gram made me feel confident I could accomplish anything."

"You strike me as a woman who feels confident wherever you are."

"I try. Gram used to tell me that trying is winning."

"Astute lady."

She smiled, remembering the sunny afternoon she'd fully understood Gram's lesson on trying. "When I was about ten, she used to let me paddle the canoe around by myself while she watched from the pier. With a life jacket, of course. I felt invincible. Too much so, I guess, because one day, I managed to tip the canoe over. When I came up for air, I was shocked Gram wasn't swimming out to save me."

He chuckled.

"All she said was, 'Don't let the canoe drift away.' Then she sat sipping her lemonade and let me try over and over to right the canoe and climb back in. When I finally succeeded, I felt like queen of the mountain."

"What a way to instill self-confidence."

"See what I mean? She believed in me enough to let me try until I could believe in myself. Does that make sense?"

"Perfect sense."

"Good. As a mother, I appreciate her even more. Things haven't been easy since my husband's death, but it's very important to me to make a good life for my boys and give them the space they need to believe in themselves. That's why I moved to the cottage. To believe in myself again. It's why having my parents here for Christmas dinner is so important."

"What do you mean?"

"I need to show them, and myself I guess, that I am getting my life together. I'm just sorry you got caught in my struggles to do it, that's all."

He frowned. "Like I said, I'm glad I can help."

He really seemed sincere about that. "I don't know what I would do without your help tonight." She sipped her chocolate.

"Enough with the gratitude, okay? Do you have insurance on the cottage?"

"Yes." She'd been so honored Gram had left the cottage to her that she'd stood up to her father the way Gram would have and insisted on buying her own insurance. It was one of her proudest moments over this past year.

"Great. The structure looks sound. You can have it looked at, see if it's worth fixing."

She frowned. "Because of the cost?"

He nodded.

What if it cost too much? She couldn't deal with that possibility right now. "Can we talk about you for a while?"

"What do you want to know?"

She thought for a moment. "You said you were very involved with finding housing for the homeless in Chicago. How did that happen?"

"Through Hope's mother."

"Oh. Was she a social worker?"

A small cloud passed over his features.

"I'm sorry. We don't need to talk about her if it's too painful."

"It's okay. To answer your question, no, she wasn't a social worker. Actually, I met Shelby when I did a series of articles to inform the public about drug addiction." His face softened. "She was a great subject…honest, strong, brave… and pregnant. And she was fighting hard to stay clean for her baby."

Alyssa frowned, not following. "You mean…Hope? She was pregnant with Hope?"

He nodded. "I helped her get off the streets and into a shelter for pregnant girls. She found a job, took good care of Hope for a few months after she was born…" He shook his head. "Shelby was the little sister I never had."

He spoke so tenderly about her. "What happened?"

"I often met them in the park to play with Hope. Such a bright little thing, and Shelby just lit up when she interacted with her. But one day, she asked me to take her baby."

A chill shook Alyssa.

"She didn't have to tell me she was going back to drugs," Ben said solemnly. "But she wouldn't listen."

"What did you do?"

"I took Hope home with me."

"Just like that?"

"I loved Hope. No way was I going to let any harm come to that sweet little baby."

Alyssa didn't know what to say. She couldn't imagine how a single man could take on the challenge of raising a child, let alone one who wasn't his own.

"I never gave up on Shelby, but we hardly saw her. She signed adoption papers. She died when Hope was two."

"I'm so sorry."

"She was such a good mother…so much potential." The futility in his voice was still there after all this time.

"So you worked to help the homeless."

"Shelby put a face on people less fortunate than me."

"So how did you discover Rainbow Lake?"

"Indirectly, Shelby was the reason for that, too. After her death, I needed a break from the city, a chance to get my head together. A buddy invited Hope and me to come here on a fishing trip with him and his family. Turned out the *Courier* was for sale. I liked the area so much that my buddy and I joked about me buying the paper and moving to give him and his family a place to stay when they came here."

"So you did?"

"Not then. Even though raising Hope in the city bothered me, housing for the homeless had become such an important part of my life that I didn't want to leave it. It took me three years of coming back for vacations. Every trip, Hope and I found something else to love about the area, and the paper was still for sale. The challenge of taking on the business end of a small newspaper as well as continuing to write intrigued me."

"What finally changed your mind?"

"I met a force of a woman named Lou at church when I was here on vacation. She was interested in doing something about the shortage of housing in the area, so I told her about my experiences in Chicago. Together, we formed a group of interested church people, and the Reclamation Committee was born."

"Reclamation Committee?"

"The plan is to reclaim old buildings and make them into as many apartments as space allows. We fix them up, keep rent low and use rent money to fund our next project."

"Pretty ambitious project for a church committee, isn't it?"

He gave a nod. "Lot slower going than we'd ever imagined, too. But we finally managed to raise enough money to buy our first building. We've gutted it. The only thing keeping us from finishing the job is coming up with enough money for supplies and appliances."

Alyssa smiled. "So you're happy with your decision to move."

He nodded enthusiastically. "I figure God wanted me here. He'd provided the place, the people, the job, the church and last but not least, the low-income housing project that sealed the deal."

"Well, I'm glad you moved here," she said sincerely.

He grinned. "So am I."

No question in her mind, Ben was a man who cared enough to put himself on the line. He cared about everybody from the homeless girl on the streets of Chicago to the baby he'd adopted as his own to the big yellow dog asleep at his feet. Apparently, he didn't look at inviting strangers into his home for the night as anything out of the ordinary.

Maybe she should relax and accept his hospitality as if meeting such an extraordinary man was something she did every day.

Following smells of bacon and fresh coffee, Alyssa trudged down the open stairs in Ben's great room. Apparently, he'd already started breakfast even though she'd told him she would do it.

Robbie cooed happily in the car seat bumping against her leg. But the cloudy sky and agitated, gray lake outside the floor-to-ceiling windows more closely matched Alyssa's mood.

Of course, her problems were no more manageable this morning than they'd been last night. What was she going to do? Was the cottage too damaged to be repaired? Heaviness settled in her chest at that thought.

She couldn't think that way. She had to make it work. And she would.

And regardless of whether the cottage could be repaired, she needed to find an inexpensive place to live. Making Cam's life insurance settlement last was crucial. So she needed to find a job and day care, which could take a while. Especially a job that would allow her as much time with her boys as possible. She blew out a breath. There was no way she'd get it all pulled together by Christmas now, was there?

Approaching the kitchen, she heard Joey's voice. She was still puzzled over his willingness to follow the big yellow dog downstairs this morning without needing her to go with him. What happened to the separation anxiety he'd been struggling with since Cam's death?

Nights had become such a heart-wrenching issue that she'd finally allowed him to sleep with her. Otherwise, he'd always ended up on her bedroom floor by morning anyway.

But last night, he'd ridden to the clinic in Ben's truck without complaint. And this morning, he was downstairs without her. She was almost afraid to read these developments as a good sign. Taking a shaky breath, she walked toward the commotion in the kitchen, the scene from the doorway stopping her in her tracks.

Ben's broad back to her, he stood at the stove in a dark blue sweater, his black hair shining in the dim glow from the skylight above. With a flourish, he scooped up a very small pancake from the griddle and flipped it into the air. "It's up, it's over and it's a safe landing for one more silver-dollar pancake with Joey's name on it," Ben announced in the excited tone of a sports commentator as he caught the pancake on a plate in his other hand.

Hope began clapping.

The dog lay at her feet, thumping his tail. He rolled friendly brown eyes at Alyssa as if this foolishness went on all the time and was nothing to get excited about.

"And it's another silver-dollar pancake taking to the air at warp speed." Ben flipped a pancake high, too high. "Whoops." He lurched to position the plate under the falling disc—and caught it.

Sitting on a stool beside Hope at the island counter, Joey

watched wide-eyed as if trying to figure out how he should react to all this exuberance.

"Coop saves another rebel from biting the dust!" Hope yelled. Laughing and clapping, she began to chant. "Go, Coop. Go, Coop."

As if taking his cue, the dog jumped up and barked loud enough to shake the house.

Robbie let out a piercing screech of outrage, then held his breath.

Ben turned from the grill, alarm and confusion written plainly on his face.

Brushing past the dog, Alyssa hurried into the kitchen and set the carrier on the island. Murmuring assurances, she snapped open the safety strap and clasped her baby to her.

Joey scrambled to stand on his stool and held Braveman up for Robbie to see. "Don't be scart, Robbie. Braveman's here."

The baby caught his breath and wailed. It was going to take more than his big brother and his superhero to convince Robbie everything was right in his world. Alyssa cuddled his tense body to her shoulder, stroking his back. Three pairs of guilty eyes watched, four if she counted the dog. Robbie's cries thinned and finally stopped.

"He was crying too hard to see Braveman, Mommy." Joey sat down. "Digger didn't mean to scare him."

"Don't worry, honey. Robbie's fine."

"I guess we got carried away, huh, Dad?"

Ben arched an eyebrow. "I hope we didn't traumatize the little guy."

"He's not used to so much excitement, that's all." Hugging Robbie close, Alyssa settled onto a stool beside Joey. "I thought you were going to let me cook breakfast."

"You have the baby to tend to. I wake up at the crack of

dawn, so I have plenty of time." He set a steaming mug of coffee in front of her. "Cream or sugar?"

"You don't need to wait on me."

"You're my guest. Cream or sugar?" he repeated.

She sighed. "Black, thanks."

"So, enjoy your coffee."

She took a sip, the robust flavor warming her as much as the temperature. "It's wonderful."

"Ben found Braveman in Gram's kitchen," Joey said.

"Don't worry, we gave Braveman a bath." Ben flashed her a grin that stirred her pulse.

Oh, please. Really? Feeling a connection with him wasn't enough? Now her pulse was responding to his smile? A man…any man…was the very last thing she wanted in her life. How would she ever learn to stand on her own with somebody rushing in to rescue her every time things got difficult? Ignoring her pulse, she focused on Joey. "Did you thank Ben?"

"Thank you."

"You're welcome." Ben turned to the griddle, scooped pancakes and bacon onto plates and set them on the island counter. "Maybe you'd rather have grown-up pancakes?"

"Absolutely not. Silver dollars sound intriguing."

"Well, eat up while they're hot." He turned back to the grill and poured batter that sizzled and sent more mouthwatering steam wafting over his shoulder.

Alyssa laid dozing Robbie into his carrier and moved him to the table, out of the line of fire but close enough to keep her eye on him.

Hope held up a glass container filled with syrup. "Everybody want maple syrup and melted butter on their pancakes?"

"Let me do that, Hope."

"I got it." Hope deftly doused everybody's pancakes with

the butter-syrup mixture, then pushed plates to Alyssa and Joey. "There you go, sport."

Joey grimaced. "I'm not sport. I'm Joey."

Alyssa settled onto the stool beside him. "Hope's just having fun with you."

Joey squinted as if trying to understand. "Like a joke?"

"Yes, like a joke." Alyssa took a bite that melted in her mouth. "These are delicious."

"Secret recipe." Ben glanced over his shoulder, his lips quirking at the corners. "Right off the Bisquick box."

He had the most disarming way about him. Strong, kind, warm. She took another bite. And another. She sipped her excellent coffee. And she watched Ben scoop pancakes and refill plates like a good host, without once allowing herself to jump up and help.

Good thing he made everything look fun and easy. A single father and yet, he'd created the coziest, most relaxed kitchen she'd ever been privileged to eat breakfast in. The kind of kitchen she wanted to make in Gram's cottage.

Provided it could be repaired. "Now that the sun is up, I need to take a look at the cottage."

"I checked it this morning," he said. "No frozen water pipes, but daylight didn't do much to improve it, I'm afraid."

"I'm going to have to hire somebody who knows construction."

"Dad knows construction."

Ben held up his hands. "Some."

"More than some, Dad," Hope scolded. "We tore down the shack that was here, and like I told you last night, Dad built our house," she said proudly.

"I mostly did the grunt stuff."

Capable and modest, too? "Do you have any idea how much money it would take to repair the cottage?"

"Mommy," Joey said timidly, "can I go outside and play with Digger?"

"We need to finish eating."

"When I'm done eating, can I? Please?"

She liked the big Lab, but she couldn't depend on him to keep Joey safe. "We need to stay inside with Robbie, honey."

Ben topped off her coffee before she even thought about doing it. "Aren't you going to eat?"

"I ate earlier." He turned to his daughter. "Hope, are you ready for church?"

"Yes. I'll go outside with him."

Alyssa doubted Joey would go with Hope.

"Can I go with Digger and Hope, Mommy?"

Alyssa blinked. What had gotten into him? He really *was* ready to break away from her? She'd be all for it, but... "Hope, you don't have to do that."

"It's cool. Digger always needs exercise in the mornings anyway."

"Would you like to go to church with us, Alyssa?" Ben asked.

Surprised by his invitation, she swallowed a bite of food. Churches were full of helpful people looking for a project—the last place she wanted to be right now. "Thanks, but no."

Ben turned to set the coffeepot on its burner.

"We don't go. To church." Why she felt the need to explain, she didn't know.

"Never?"

"Not for a while." She had no idea how she'd attend a church service without crying all the way through it. Letting her answer suffice, she focused on Joey. "We'll have to get your mittens and hat from the car."

"I'll get them," Hope offered.

"Do you mind?"

Frowning at Alyssa, Hope shook her head. "I'm going outside anyway."

Alyssa tried to remember where she'd put her keys, alarm prickling her neck. "I don't remember locking the car last night."

"Nobody locks up in Rainbow Lake," Ben assured her.

She sighed, relieved. In a different place, she could have easily had her car and U-Haul stolen. Then where would she be?

Joey scrambled to his knees on his stool and leaned to whisper in her ear. "Can I say a joke to Hope?"

Steadying him, she nodded, wondering what he would come up with.

He sat back down and hurriedly finished his last pancake. Apparently, he needed time to hatch his joke. "I'm full, Mommy. Can I go outside now?"

Alyssa glanced at his empty plate. "Good job. You must promise to do what Hope says."

"I promise." He jumped off his stool and bolted.

Gulping down the last of her pancakes, Hope climbed off her stool and followed him. "Wait up, dude. I'll get a ball for Dig to chase."

"Okay, pancake head." Joey peered at Hope as if waiting for her reaction.

She laughed. "Good one, Joey."

He burst into hilarious laughter as if he'd just said the cleverest thing in the world.

Alyssa smiled. It appeared her son had figured out what teasing was and felt comfortable enough to try it out for himself. That, along with his willingness to leave her side, was all adding up to a major breakthrough. And hearing him laugh was priceless.

Ben brought his coffee and sat on the stool one over from her. "Kids are pretty cool, aren't they?"

"They are. I appreciate your making him feel included."

He gave her a thoughtful look.

The kids and dog slammed out the door.

Pulse humming, Alyssa dragged her gaze from Ben's dark eyes and brushed a crumb from her wool slacks. She enjoyed sipping coffee with this attractive, extraordinary man in his charming kitchen and chatting about their children.

She'd forgotten what it was like to simply enjoy a man's company. Not that she wanted more than that. Her mind returned to her questions. "Can you give me an idea what it might take to repair the cottage?"

He uneasily met her eyes. "Lumber to fix the roof and bricks for the chimney will run several hundred dollars."

She brightened a bit. "Several hundred dollars doesn't sound too bad."

"Add labor. I'm sure the place will have to be treated to get rid of the smoke stench, and at least some of the drywall will have to be replaced before it's painted. You might have to update the wiring and put in a new furnace and ductwork. It could get pretty expensive."

A sick feeling washing over her, she set down her coffee.

"Trouble is, you'll spend a considerable amount of money and still have an old, inefficient cottage."

"But if I can afford to fix it, it will *still* be my gram's cottage."

He nodded. "It will at that."

"Hey, Coop," a man's voice boomed as the back door slammed again.

Alyssa turned in her stool to see a tall, muscular man with eyes as black as his hair emerge from the laundry room with a vase of beautiful yellow mums in one hand and a casserole in the other.

"Do I smell pancakes?" the man asked.

"Sure do. Alyssa Douglas, this is Tony Stefano." Ben got up and walked behind the island counter.

"Nice to meet you, Tony," she said.

His dark eyes assessed her. "Actually, we've met. Your last name was Bradley then. And you wore pigtails when I mowed the grass for your grandmother in the summers."

"Your golden retriever used to wait for you?"

"Kip." Tony handed the vase of flowers to Alyssa. "My wife, Maggie, sent these for you. She owns the greenhouse south of town. She's singing in the choir for both services this morning, but she said to tell you she's sorry for the fire."

"They're beautiful." Apparently, Tony's wife was one of those busy church ladies. Alyssa smelled the subtle scent of the blossoms and set them on the counter. "But how did you find out—"

"News travels fast when people hear the fire siren. Anyway, my grandmother sent her eggplant Parmesan and told me to tell you she's sorry about the fire, too." He set the casserole on the island counter.

Flowers *and* casseroles? The fire had already earmarked her as the needy one. Not the way to introduce herself to the community.

"Coop can cook, but his repertoire is limited."

"Not everybody's an expert in the kitchen like you are. Tony can cook with the best." Ben set a steaming mug of coffee on the counter in front of his friend. "Want some pancakes?"

"No, thanks." Tony took a long, slow sip. "*Nonna* keeps me as well fed as she keeps Maggie."

"Tony and Maggie have a daughter, Christa, and they're expecting a baby around Christmas," Ben explained.

"How wonderful."

Tony beamed. "We can't wait." He strode over to assess Robbie asleep in his car seat on the table. "How old?"

"Three months."

"He's amazing. I assume the blond kid I met outside belongs to you, too?"

She nodded. "Joey just turned four."

"Nice family. Fortunate woman."

"Yes," she agreed, "I am."

"Tony owns Stefano Construction Company," Ben explained. "I asked him to bring a tarp and help me stretch it over your cottage. Snow's on the way. And the tarp will protect your place for the winter. You can have the damaged stuff cleaned out and the cottage repaired in the spring, if that's what you decide to do."

"Spring?" She looked from Ben to Tony in alarm. "There's no way I can fix it and live there this winter?"

The men looked at her as if she wasn't making sense.

"Have you ever spent a winter in northern Wisconsin?" Tony asked.

"I've lived in Madison for five years. Winters are cold there, too."

"Your grandmother never spent winters in her cottage. It doesn't even have storm windows," Ben pointed out. "Probably not much insulation either."

"Won't the furnace and fireplace keep the cottage warm enough?"

Ben shook his head. "The furnace is probably ancient and inefficient. You could never burn enough wood to keep the place warm."

"You could winterize it," Tony said. "It's not that big, so it wouldn't cost a ton more to do it while the rest of the work is going on."

"You said last night that you have insurance on it, right?" Ben asked.

"Yes, I do."

"So hire Tony to fix up the place come spring, and bring

your kids next summer to enjoy the lake. It only makes sense for you to go back to Madison for the winter."

"I don't have a place to live in Madison."

"But you know your way around there. And you have friends to help you out there."

She shook her head. "Friends have been helping me out ever since Cam died. I don't want to impose on them any longer. Besides, moving to Rainbow Lake was a huge decision." Sure, Gram's cottage offered free rent, but more importantly, it gave her the emotional support and inspiration she needed to grow into the strong, independent woman she wanted to become. She wasn't going to throw that away and run back to Madison with her hand out.

Hearing barking and kids' squeals outside, she got up and walked to the window to make sure Joey was okay.

Digger chased a ball across the brown, dormant grass, barking with abandon. Arms waving wildly, Joey ran after the dog, squealing and laughing for all he was worth.

Ben chuckled over her shoulder. "Joey and Digger look like somebody forgot to lock the gate."

Tears clouding her vision, Alyssa pressed her fingers to her lips to stifle a sob. *This* was what her son needed. What she needed, too. No question in her mind, she'd made the right decision. "Tony, I want to hire you now, not in the spring. How long do you think it would take you to fix and winterize the cottage?"

Silence for a couple beats. The men were probably exchanging looks.

"Two to three weeks," Tony answered.

He'd have it done before Christmas? She turned to them. "That's terrific. I'll find someplace to rent until then. What kind of down payment do you need?"

"I'll work up an estimate and let you know." He glanced at his watch. "Coop, we'd better get moving. I'll get the tarp out of the truck." He strode out of the room, the back door soon closing.

"You sure you want to go ahead with this?" Ben asked.

"Absolutely. Coming here is a major step in taking charge of my life. I can't crumble at the first obstacle."

"You sure you can't take charge of your life in Madison?"

"With friends scrambling to make sure things are easy for me? And my parents calling them to check on me? I know they're worried about us, but I'm doing okay now. I just need space to figure things out for myself. It's even possible I could be established by Christmas, so I can show my parents I can take care of my little family on my own."

"Why is a Christmas deadline so important?"

"It's just that…through the darkest times this past year, I dreamed of preparing a dinner with Gram. Turkey and all the trimmings, you know? Everybody sharing it around her table. But she died this past spring." She stopped a moment to get her emotions under control before she went on.

"When she left me the cottage, I began to dream of starting over there. And because Christmas is the next time I'll see my parents…"

"You plan to show them you're okay and put their minds at ease."

"Exactly."

"Well, I hope you can make it work out the way you want it to." He strode for the laundry room. "Better help Tony with that tarp if we're going to make it to church."

Chapter Four

Alyssa's windshield wipers whirred, losing their battle to keep up with falling snow. She'd been out looking for a temporary place to live for the two to three weeks Tony estimated it would take to fix the cottage. All she needed were a couple of furnished rooms for her and the boys. Of course, she'd thought she'd be successful and be back at Ben's to pick up her U-Haul by now.

But the three rentals she'd found listed in the *Courier* had been awful. Worse than awful. Running the addresses by Ben might have saved her some time, but she'd made him and Hope late for church as it was. She certainly wasn't going to hold them up any longer. Apparently, housing was as scarce in the area as Ben said it was.

She peered through the snowy haze, looking for the turnoff onto Rainbow Lake Road. With no streetlights, the snow-covered road ahead blended with the countryside around her. She hadn't seen another car for ages. Everybody else had enough sense to get off the roads in weather like this. And she would, too, as soon as she wound her way to the right one.

She hated going back to Ben's without a place to live, but she didn't have anywhere else to go. So once again, she

would have to rely on his help. She shook her head, defeat
pressing her down.

She needed to figure out a way to pay him back. Cleaning, cooking. Anything. Gripping the steering wheel until
her fingers ached, she took a curve.

Suddenly, her car spun around and slid for the ditch. She
held the wheel steady, even remembered to touch the brake
lightly instead of stomping it. But the car ended up in the
snow-filled ditch just the same.

"What happened, Mommy?" Joey sounded surprised.

She blew out a breath. "We slid on the ice, honey." Thankfully, she'd been driving slowly. Slamming the car in Park,
she quickly unsnapped her seat belt and scrambled to her
knees to peer at her children in their car seats in the back.
"You okay?"

Joey nodded.

"Good." She watched Robbie stretch and try to open his
eyes, then settle back to sleep. "The most important thing
is that everybody's okay, right?"

Joey nodded again.

Settling behind the wheel, she threw her frustration into
every trick she knew to get the car out of the ditch. But it
wouldn't budge. The incline and the awkward angle told
her there was no way she would escape without a tow. She
groaned.

"Daddy would know what to do."

"Yes, honey, he would." One of the things she missed
most about Cam was his take-charge attitude. Tears threat-
ened. She brushed them away. What good would tears do?
If she'd relied on herself instead of depending on Cam for
so many things, she'd know what to do, too.

"Let's call Ben."

She almost groaned again, but she didn't want to upset
Joey. Needing to stay with Ben for another night wasn't

bad enough. Now she needed him to pull her car out of the ditch? But wait—her cell had gotten wrecked in the fire. She let the ramifications of that bit of information seep through her mind.

What *was* she going to do?

"Ben will come and help us, Mommy. I know he will."

She winced. "My phone got broken in the fire. And Ben doesn't know where we are."

"He will look for us," Joey offered matter-of-factly.

Ben had done enough. She certainly didn't expect him to be out on these roads searching for them. With a heavy sigh, she turned to scan the shifting landscape through the windshield and spotted a light in the sky. A yard light? The end of a big barn took shape in the haze, and she slowly made out a two-story house close by. Was it a working farm with people who could lend her a phone? Why else would they have a light?

But she couldn't leave the boys in the car. She'd have to take them through the blizzard with her. This just got better and better. She turned off the motor, shoved open her door and stepped into a snowbank to her knees.

Wind pelting her with wet snow, she crawled in the back alongside Robbie's car seat and pulled the door shut behind her. She dug in her giant tote on the floor and handed Joey his mittens and scarf, then unsnapped his seat belt. "Put your boots back on, okay?"

"What are we gonna do?"

"We're going to walk to that farmhouse and get help."

"Like a 'venture?"

"That's right. Like an adventure." Kneeling on the seat, she grabbed an extra blanket from the Escalade's rear section.

"Is this the right one?" Joey looked up from jamming his right foot into his left boot.

She glanced over from struggling to get sleeping Robbie into his snowsuit and shook her head.

Joey gave a sigh of discouragement. "We need Ben to come and help us."

Apparently, Ben was Joey's new superhero. At the rate she was going, she'd never fill that role in her child's life, would she? "Just pull off your boot and put it on the other foot, okay?"

"I need help, Mommy."

"We need to learn to help ourselves, honey. I'm sure you can do it."

He sighed. "Like the little engine?"

"Just like the little engine."

He set to work. "I think I can, I think I can...."

By the time she got the boys and herself bundled up enough to face the blizzard, it felt like a major achievement to finally push open the door and climb out with Robbie in his carrier. "Come on, Joey."

Gripping Braveman in his mitten, Joey scrambled out, blinking against the biting snow.

She slammed the door. Grasping Joey's hand, she headed for the house. It was hard going through the drifts, especially for Joey. "You're doing great," she encouraged.

"Braveman knows the way."

"Well, that's good." The closer they got to the house, the more run-down it looked. Visions of scary houses in too many thriller movies nudged her mind. But this was Rainbow Lake country. Hadn't Ben said people didn't even lock doors around here?

She couldn't see any lights. What would she do if nobody was home? What if nobody even lived there?

But as she rounded the side of the structure, a dim glow spilled out on the snow. Gratefully climbing the steps of the wraparound porch, she let go of Joey's hand to knock on the door with knuckles numb from the cold.

No sound came from inside.

She banged on the door with her fist. "Is anybody home?" she yelled.

Robbie began to protest.

She kept right on pounding. *Come on, answer the door. We're freezing out here.*

Finally, she stopped, pushed her wet, windblown hair from her eyes and tried to face the possibility that for whatever reason, nobody was going to answer her knock.

"Maybe they're sleeping," Joey said.

She looked down at her son, the trust in his wide eyes spurring her into action. She set up pounding the door again. "Please open your door. I have two young children. Are you going to let us freeze on your doorstep?"

The door creaked open a crack.

"I'm sorry to bother you, but my car slid into the ditch."

"You shouldn't be out in this storm," a crotchety man's voice grumbled through the crack in the door.

All Alyssa could make out in the shadowy light inside was one aged eye behind a glass lens.

"Who's with you?" the man demanded.

"My baby and my little boy. Do you think I could bring them inside? It's very cold out here."

"How do I know you're not going to rob me?"

From the looks of the place, what could the man possibly have to steal?

Robbie's fussing erupted into crying.

She hunted for his pacifier in the blankets and gave it to him. "Do you have a phone? That's all we want. I promise."

"Who you want to call?" the crackly voice asked.

"Ben Cooper…he lives on Rainbow Lake."

"The guy that bought the *Courier?*"

"The town newspaper?"

"I read his paper. Don't know Ben Cooper, though."

Robbie's cries erupted, definitely cries of hunger by now.

"My brother is cold, and I need to go potty," Joey contributed.

Desperate to get her children out of the wind, if only for a few minutes, Alyssa groped for anything she could think of to gain entrance into the man's inner sanctum. He appeared to have lived here forever, yet he didn't know Ben.... "Emma and Charles Bradley were my grandparents."

The door opened a foot or so, and the ancient man in overalls, plaid flannel shirt and a white beard glowered at crying Robbie, then down at Joey. "Emma and Charlie and me and my late wife go way back."

Thank you, Gram and Gramps. Alyssa located the pacifier again and tried to get Robbie to take it.

The old man looked Alyssa in the eye. "Where's your husband?"

"My husband died." Finally, she got Robbie to accept the pacifier.

Joey danced in place. "Can I use your bathroom… please?"

The man grunted. "Well, come in, then."

Alyssa let out a relieved breath. Guiding Joey inside, she followed him into a very old, outdated kitchen. Faded wallpaper in a teakettle theme, wall-hanging sink, big, black-and-silver wood-burning stove. The room was as different from Ben's modern, cozy kitchen as it could possibly be. But it was warm and everything they needed right now. "I'm Alyssa Douglas."

"Zebadiah Krentz." Closing the door, the man peered down at Joey. "What's your name?"

Joey looked up at her through steamed glasses, his nose wrinkling. "Clean slution?"

She sniffed the pine scent. "That's right. Can you tell Mr. Krentz your name?" she encouraged.

"Joseph Bradley Douglas, like my grampa," he said without looking at the old man.

"Joseph Bradley is your grampa?"

Nodding, Joey handed his glasses to Alyssa and hopped on one foot. "Can I use your potty? Please?"

The old man slowly turned and pointed an arthritic finger. "It's in there. Don't forget to flush."

"I won't." Squinting to see across the room, Joey took off for the bathroom.

Alyssa followed him and pulled the bathroom door partially closed to give him privacy. She stood just outside to make sure he didn't get into trouble.

"Joseph Bradley, Emma and Charlie's boy?" Mr. Krentz asked.

"Yes."

"Joseph here, too?"

"My father?"

"Joseph Bradley's your dad?"

"Yes. But he's in Washington right now. He's a U.S. senator."

Robbie spit out his pacifier and began crying in earnest. She tried to get him to accept it one more time.

"I'd like to see Joseph again. That lad worked hard for me."

"In the Senate?" Giving up with the pacifier, she clasped Robbie to her shoulder and rubbed his back to try to calm him.

"The Senate? No. Probably works hard there, too. But he used to work his tail off helping me bring in the hay. Emma and Charlie raised that boy right."

Alyssa smiled, amazed at how pleased she was to find someone connected to her father and grandparents.

"I taught Charlie a thing or two about fishing way back when. Too bad he had to leave us so soon." Mr. Krentz slowly shook his head. "Then my Viola."

Alyssa remembered a Viola being a friend of Gram. She'd thought it was so cool to be named for a flower. And she'd met this man, too, hadn't she? "I'm sorry."

"Yeah, well…thanks." He cleared his throat. "Your gramma Emma did her best to keep me goin' when she was here during the summers. Never gave up on me or that little cottage of hers, no matter how bad it got. Tough lady, your grandmother."

"Yes, she was."

The toilet flushed.

Robbie was getting more upset by the second. She was going to have to nurse him, but she couldn't imagine Zebadiah Krentz taking *that* well. She excused herself and hurried into the bathroom. Ten minutes later, she emerged with Joey wearing his glasses again and a quiet, satisfied Robbie dozing in his carrier.

The old man shuffled around, mopping the worn linoleum floor.

"I'm sorry we tracked snow into your home," she apologized.

"That's what this mop is for."

Well, he had a point there. "If I can use your phone to call Ben, we'll soon be out of your way."

He leaned the mop against the wall, took a green-and-black plaid mackinaw from a metal hook and struggled into it. "Did you wreck your car when you slid into the ditch?"

"It seems fine. But it's pretty stuck. I'm sure it will have to be towed out."

He pulled a heavy, hand-knit cap down over his ears and wrapped a scarf around his neck, beard and half his face. "While I get my tractor out of the machine shed, you and your little 'uns walk down and meet me at your car. Can you do that?"

"You'll freeze on a tractor in this blizzard." Now, she was depending on a very old man to rescue her? She glanced around for a phone, spotting an old rotary version on the kitchen counter. "Maybe Ben can bring his truck."

"No need for him to come out on a night like this. If we need him, we can always call him later."

What if he got pneumonia or something? "I don't think you should go out there, Mr. Krentz."

"Name's Zebadiah to Charlie and Emma's kin. And just how am I gonna get that car of yours out of the ditch without going out there? Ain't no need to thank me neither. At least not until I get you pulled out and on your way home."

"Have you heard from Alyssa?" Tension knotting his gut, Coop pulled onto the narrow shoulder and peered around the flashing windshield wipers. He could barely see through the blinding snow.

"Not a word." Hope's voice on the speakerphone sounded as worried as he felt. "What if they're stuck in a snowbank someplace, Dad? And they run out of gas?"

His concern, too. One of many. "Alyssa has lived in Wisconsin long enough to know she needs to keep her gas tank full to make sure they stay warm if they get stalled." At least, that was what he'd been telling himself.

"They must be scared."

He couldn't let himself think about that. "Adults are used to handling all kinds of things, Hope. Try to pray, okay?"

"I am. You coming home soon? TV is warning people off the roads. They say our area is going to get buried." She sounded more upset with each word.

Unfortunately, praying wasn't calming her down any more than it was calming him. "I'm near Rainbow Lake

Road right now, but I have a couple more roads to check. Remember, all-wheel drive is my secret weapon."

"Does Alyssa have it?"

Unfortunately, no. He'd looked. "She didn't need it in the city."

"Just come home, okay?"

"Roger that. I'm about out of places to look, so I won't be long." He clicked off, a jolt of red in the bleak landscape riveting his attention. Taillights? Turning onto Rainbow Lake Road?

He threw his truck into gear and eased back onto the road. Accelerating, he took the turn, speeding up as much as he dared to get a better look at the slow-moving vehicle shrouded in snow. He was sweating by the time he determined the vehicle was, in fact, Alyssa's Escalade. He breathed a silent thank-you.

When she pulled into his driveway, he roared to a stop, jumped from his truck and raced to her car.

She opened the door and stepped out, her hair blowing wildly around her face.

He stopped in front of her, squelching the impulse to pull her into his arms. She looked exhausted and as tense as he was. "You all right?"

"Yes." Holding her hair back with her hand, she gave him a strained look. "A little worse for wear, that's all."

"I've been looking everywhere for you."

"I'm so sorry. You shouldn't have gone out in this storm. We slid off the road."

"You—" He swiped his hand across his face, trying to shut out the worst-case scenarios his mind fed him.

"And we didn't find a place to rent either."

He could have told her there was nothing worth renting in the area if she'd asked. "You and your guys are safe now. That's all that matters." He'd never meant anything more.

But thoughts of what could have happened to them out there in the boonies hammered at him while he helped her inside…while she and Joey told Hope and him what had happened…while she tucked the baby in for a nap….

Needing to keep busy, Coop decided an early supper would make up for missing lunch. He left Hope teaching Joey a computer game and strode for the kitchen. Digger looked up from his post at Joey's feet, ready for action if it was called for. Coop gave him a "stay" hand, and Dig settled back down with a low groan.

Coop popped Tony's grandmother's casserole into the freezer for another day and went to work collecting makings for a couple pizzas. He pulverized a clove of garlic and scooped it into a sauté pan to sizzle with onion and butter, the wonderful smell making his stomach growl in anticipation.

"It smells good in here." Alyssa glided into the room in a bluish-green, terry outfit that molded to her curves as if it had been tailored just for her. Judging from her stylish clothes, it probably had.

And here she was, back in his kitchen, and he felt more responsible for her and her boys than ever. "It's a good thing Krentz let you in."

"He didn't want to. He was afraid we'd steal from him."

"People say he's been holed up on that farm for years. He has groceries delivered. Money's always on the porch, but no sign of Zebadiah." Coop pummeled dough on the breadboard, the activity only serving to build more tension in his muscles.

"He knew my grandparents. He said my father used to help him bring in his hay. What made him so reclusive?"

He paused to let the dough rest a couple minutes. "People say he never was very social, but they started seeing even less of him after his wife died."

"He mentioned that Gram did her best to keep him going. Maybe he meant she encouraged him to get out of the house." She walked to the refrigerator. "I'll make a salad to go with the pizza, okay?"

"Great. Bowls are in the lower cupboard." He ripped the dough in two, shoved it onto pizza pans and jabbed the crusts to fit.

"Do you always make pizzas from scratch?"

"My dad and I lived on fast food and frozen pizzas while I was growing up. I can't stand them. Besides, I figure anything that doesn't have preservatives and mysterious ingredients I can't pronounce should be healthier for Hope, too, right?"

"I'm sure you're right." She washed romaine under the faucet. "Do you have any idea where I might find a short-term rental?"

"Eau Claire would be the closest."

"Eau Claire? Do you think it will be expensive to rent there?"

"I don't know, but it's a small city that should have everything you need." Maybe then, he could stop worrying about her and her boys.

"I'll drive there in the morning."

"You can't go tomorrow."

Drying the lettuce with paper towels, she gave him a questioning look.

"They're predicting snow most of the night. Roads will be terrible tomorrow." Anyway, Eau Claire might fit her needs, but how safe would they be there? After all, it was a city with all the risks and dangers of any metropolitan area. He rubbed his jaw. Since when had he turned cityphobic? Apparently, since Alyssa and her boys had gotten lost in the snowstorm.

He turned to stir the browned garlic and onion into the

sauce simmering on the stove, then dumped it onto the dough. "Where did you live in Madison?"

"We bought a lovely home on Lake Mendota."

"Were you able to sell it during the market downturn?"

"No." She tore lettuce into a bowl. "The bank foreclosed and we had to vacate."

She was in worse financial shape than he'd thought. "That's why you came to Rainbow Lake earlier than you'd planned?"

She nodded. "I was able to sell most of my furniture, which was good. But everything I own is in that U-Haul, so I'll need to rent a furnished place."

More expense. "Tony's time frame on the cottage is two to three weeks, right?"

"Yes. I hired him to winterize and install a new furnace, too."

"Will you have enough to live on in the meantime?"

"I'll be fine. Insurance should cover a lot of the cottage repairs, and I have Cam's small life insurance policy. I need to find a job. But fixing the cottage makes more sense than paying rent for the long term. And living there is very important to me."

She'd made her point on that. Grating cheese as if he had a grudge against it, he thought about how helpless he'd felt when he couldn't find them in the blizzard. He sure didn't need a repeat. Which meant keeping them under his watchful eye, didn't it? He turned back to her. "Why don't you stay here until your place is ready?"

She paused the knife and peered at him. "Live with you? You've already done too much, Ben. You don't even know me."

"I trust you not to run off with the family silver, provided we had some."

"I don't feel comfortable accepting so much from you."

"You need help right now. And I'm able to give it. Simple as that."

"Not really. I need to figure out how to help myself."

"And you will. But while you do that, you need a safe place for your boys, right?"

She sighed. "Of course, you're right, but—"

"There are no buts where your boys are concerned, are there?"

She shook her head. "But two to three weeks with a woman and two kids underfoot? Have you thought about that?"

The woman would be more of a challenge than the kids. But there was no relationship involved, nor was he looking for one. At least, not until Hope was on her own. He'd never risk her.

But Alyssa was essentially a stranger who needed help, and helping people was a big part of who he was as a man and a Christian. He couldn't turn her and her boys away. "Hope and I are pretty flexible."

"Have you talked to her about this?"

"She'll love the idea."

"Are you sure?"

"Absolutely."

"What will your friends think?"

They'd probably think he'd lost his mind, but they'd support him anyway. "They'll take it in stride."

"Because they already know your heart's too big for your own good?"

"Not true. Actually, you'd be doing me a favor by staying."

She raised her eyebrow. "Right."

"You will." His gaze locked with hers. "I'll sleep a whole lot better if I know you and your boys are all right."

Frowning, she turned back to finish the salad, deep in thought.

After adding finishing touches to the pizzas, he picked them up, shoved them into the oven and turned to her again.

She met his eyes. "I need to pay rent."

"Absolutely not."

"Why not? I'd have to pay rent if I found someplace else to live."

"I don't need rent. Put your money into the cottage."

She jammed her hands on her hips as if taking a stand. "Then I insist on buying groceries and cooking and doing the cleaning."

"No." He frowned. "You don't have many options, Alyssa. Just take me up on my offer."

"Not unless you let me buy groceries and cook and clean."

He narrowed his eyes.

"I don't want charity."

"Charity?" He shook his head. "Are you kidding? We all need help once in a while. But okay, if you want to chip in on groceries and cook and clean, fine. But I'll cook breakfast."

She narrowed her eyes.

He raised his hands to stop her protest. "While you take care of the baby in the mornings. I always get up at the crack of dawn anyway. I'll leave dinner to you."

She gave him a smile, apparently satisfied with the deal.

The warmth in her smile made his breath hitch. Oh, yeah. The woman would be a challenge, all right. He liked her. Probably a good thing because they'd be living in the same house. He just couldn't fall for her, that was all.

But their arrangement would be for only two or three weeks. How hard could it be?

Chapter Five

Opening the blind in Ben's guest room early next morning, a shot of light bedazzled Alyssa. She blinked through the blaze of white. The lake lay dark and unfrozen, but a flowing blanket of fluff and sparkle covered everything else. Even the stark limbs of trees along the lakefront were clothed in marshmallow softness. It looked like a brand-new world.

But here she was, relying on Ben for a place to live until the cottage was ready for occupancy. She took a deep breath.

Robbie cooed softly.

She turned from the window and gazed at her baby in the middle of the queen bed, his attention riveted on capturing his fist in his mouth.

Smiling at his determination, Alyssa turned her thoughts again to her situation. At least Ben had agreed to accept her help with groceries and cooking and cleaning, which made her feel a little less of a burden. And she was going to hold him to it despite his disarming smile.

It would definitely be harder to ignore when she'd be seeing him every day and evening until the cottage was ready. Of course, she could do it. And maybe along the way, she'd find some way to repay him for all his help. She hoped so.

Meanwhile, she'd have the day to herself while he went to work and Hope to school.

It would give her a chance to get grounded, organize a grocery list, a cleaning schedule and get started. Maybe being productive would help her feel less of a failure. Didn't she do some of her best thinking while cleaning?

She could work out a strategy to find a job, too. Then when the cottage was ready, she could concentrate on getting settled before her parents' Christmas visit. "Don't give up on me, sweetie. I'll get it together yet."

Robbie gave her a watery grin.

She scooped him up and hugged him, his warm little body and just-bathed scent comforting. Joey had gotten himself dressed and left a few minutes earlier to find Digger. She still couldn't help being amazed at how comfortable he felt here. But she'd better check on him to make sure he wasn't getting into something he shouldn't.

A soft knock on the bedroom door broke into her thoughts. "Yes?"

"Joey said you and the baby were awake." Hope's voice filtered through the door.

"Come in, Hope."

The girl pushed into the room in jeans and an oversize, black sweatshirt, probably her dad's. Was that the way she dressed for school?

"I was just going downstairs to check on Joey," Alyssa said.

"Dad's giving him breakfast."

Of course, he was.

Winding her arms behind her, Hope shifted from one bare foot to the other as if she had something on her mind.

Robbie squealed softly, apparently wanting to be noticed.

"Hi, Robbie." Hope reached out to grasp his hand. "How are you?"

His smile faded.

"He's holding on to my finger really tight." Hope looked up at Alyssa.

"He has quite a grip, hasn't he?"

Hope nodded. "I'm taking a babysitting class in school."

"That's a great idea. Do you babysit?"

"Dad thinks I'm still too young for that much responsibility, but he's letting me take care of little kids once a month in the church nursery. With that and the class, I figure I'll know what I'm doing when Dad decides I'm old enough."

"Good plan."

"You like my finger, don't you?" Hope asked. "Do you think I can hold him sometime?"

Robbie seemed fascinated with Hope. "Do you want to sit on the bed and hold him now?"

"Really?" Hope's expressive face breaking into a smile, she quickly moved to the bed and sat down.

Alyssa bent and placed her baby in the girl's outstretched arms.

"Hi, Robbie." Hope smiled enthusiastically.

Robbie gave Hope a startled look. His face scrunched up.

Oh, no.

He burst into a heart-wrenching wail.

Hope shoved him back to his mother and stood up.

Bringing her baby to her shoulder, Alyssa patted his back to reassure him. He immediately stopped crying and snuffled into her neck. Apparently, he'd decided he preferred Mommy.

"He hates me." Hope looked on the verge of tears herself.

"He doesn't hate you," Alyssa assured. "He doesn't know you yet, but he will. And you can hold him then, okay?"

Hope twisted her pixie face. "Maybe he can tell I'm like my mother. She didn't think being a mom was so great."

Alyssa focused her attention on the girl. "Do you remember her?"

She shook her head. "She didn't come around much 'cause she did drugs."

"I'm so sorry."

Hope shifted to her other foot. "I figure if she liked being my mom, she woulda stayed off drugs."

How awful for the poor girl to think she hadn't been valuable to her own mother. Maybe she could help her understand. "Hope, addiction is an illness that usually takes help to control. Maybe your mother wasn't able to get the help she needed."

"Dad made her go to rehab. She stopped using before I was born and for a few months after."

"It probably took everything she had to stay off drugs so she wouldn't harm you. You must have been very important to her."

"If I was, she shoulda stayed off drugs and taken care of me."

Alyssa had to admit she couldn't imagine a mother choosing to do something that would keep her from caring for her child. "Have you asked your dad about that?"

"He says she used drugs to forget the bad things that happened when she was growing up in foster care."

"I'm sorry."

"That's probably where I would have ended up, too—foster care—if Dad hadn't adopted me."

"But he did. And he loves you very much."

"I know. He always says I'm part of him."

Alyssa smiled. The more she got to know Hope, the more convinced she was that Ben was doing a remarkable job with his daughter. With Robbie beginning to fuss, Alyssa patted his back.

He immediately rewarded her with a loud burp.

Hope giggled. "He's weird."

Alyssa smiled.

"You know, Dad did everything he could to save my mother, but it just didn't work."

"I'm sure he did. He's a very compassionate and strong man."

Something in Hope's expression seemed to close up. She took a deep breath. "Don't do anything to hurt him."

Alyssa heard the warning in the girl's tone. "I'd never hurt him, Hope. Nor you."

Hope looked at the floor. "Just don't. That's all I'm saying." She turned on her heel and walked out of the room.

Alyssa frowned. What made Hope think she needed to warn her about her father? Had she sensed the connection Alyssa felt with Ben? Did she see her as a threat? Did she resent his helping her?

At dinner last night, Hope hadn't been as excited as Joey was about their staying here, but she'd seemed okay with it. Had she just been hesitant to object? Or had she changed her mind?

Alyssa needed to talk to Ben about his daughter's concerns. Perhaps she and her boys would be moving to Eau Claire after all.

Coop looked up from the large roast he was searing to see Alyssa, standing in the early-morning light with the baby in her arms. A beautiful picture. But the pinched tension around her eyes caught his attention. "Sleep well?"

"You agreed to let me cook."

"Wait a minute. Not breakfast, remember?"

She looked startled to realize he had guests.

"You remember Max and Liz Chandler, the EMTs the other night?" Coop reminded.

"Of course. Thank you so much for your help."

"You're very welcome," Max and Liz said in unison.

"Where's Joey?" Alyssa asked.

"He and Digger and Hope are building a snowman," Coop answered. "He ate a quick breakfast first, though."

"Hope told me. Doesn't she have to leave soon for school?"

Definitely an edge in her voice. *The stress of the past few days must be catching up to her.* "School's closed. Everything's closed. We had two feet of snow last night. We're officially snowed in."

"Oh. It seems too early for that much snow."

"It happens. More often than you might think." Coop turned the large roast and smiled at the baby. "Morning, Robbie."

The little guy gave him a sober stare.

"He's not sure about me yet. I remember Hope at that age. Wouldn't let anybody near her but her mother." He poured a mug of coffee and set it on the island for Alyssa. Maybe a jolt of caffeine would help her feel better.

She shook her head. "Please don't wait on me, okay?"

He frowned. She really was tense this morning.

Max raised his coffee mug to greet Alyssa. "We lost power, so we rode our snowmobile over. Coop's good enough to share his generator."

"We seldom lose power in town, but we did this time." Liz climbed off her stool and chucked Robbie on the cheek. "He looks the picture of health."

"He's doing fine." Alyssa laid him in his carrier on the table and strapped him in.

"We don't have many fires," Liz went on. "I wish the ones we did have all turned out as well as yours. Coop says you and the boys will be staying with him while Tony gets your cottage ready."

"Yes." Alyssa threw a glance Coop's way.

He hoped she wasn't worrying they'd think she was a charity case. Where had she gotten that idea anyway? No question in his mind, asking her to stay had been the right thing to do. It had been the only thing under the circumstances. "Hungry?"

"You're waiting on me again." Looking as grumpy as she sounded, Alyssa settled on a stool at the counter and reached for the coffee he'd put there.

He couldn't wait for her to drink it. Caffeine *always* helped. "Well, breakfast's in the warming oven whenever you're ready for it."

Maybe, while they were talking about food… "I'll be very grateful if you give Hope some pointers on cooking. I've tried, but she says I'm too bossy."

Her eyebrows arched, and she let out a little laugh. "Too bossy?"

"She could have a point about that, Coop," Max said with a grin. "I mean you do seem to think you can single-handedly fix any problem the Reclamation Committee—"

"Okay, okay." Coop smiled at Alyssa, hoping she didn't see him as a *total* dictator. "It would really help me out."

"I'd love to teach her a few simple recipes. But have you run the idea by her?"

"She'll love it."

Alyssa frowned. "Maybe you should ask her first."

What was the problem?

"She's right, Coop," Liz said. "Hope's twelve. By that age, Jess and Clarissa expected to be consulted about things."

"It made for a much happier home," Max chipped in.

He'd heard enough from Max. Coop removed the large roast from the heat and placed it in the oven. "If Hope wants something, she isn't shy about telling me."

"Provided she knows what she wants." Max contributed. "One day, the twins were blurting out whatever came into their minds. Seemed like overnight, they turned into silent land mines. If I hadn't had Liz to guide me, I would have been lost."

"Land mines? Thanks, Max. That makes me feel a lot better."

Everybody laughed.

"Liz, I thought you looked familiar," Alyssa said. "I just put it together. I remember playing with Jessie and Clarissa in the summers."

Liz nodded. "You had a great time together."

"Yes, we did." Alyssa turned to Coop. "May I talk with you for a few minutes?"

"Sure." Maybe she'd tell him what was bothering her. He glanced at Liz and Max. "Help yourselves to more coffee."

Alyssa led the way into the great room and crossed to the fireplace before she turned to face him. "I don't think Hope is happy about our staying with you."

"Are you kidding? She was fine with it at supper last night."

"Everything seemed all right then." She frowned. "But this morning she came to my room. After we got to know each other a bit, she warned me not to hurt you."

What? If Hope was concerned, why hadn't she talked to him instead of Alyssa? "I'm sorry. I'll talk to her."

"I don't want her to be unhappy about our being here."

He shook his head. "I don't think she is."

"I can look for a place in Eau Claire tomorrow."

"There's no need to remake that decision. I'll talk to Hope as soon as I get a chance. She'll be fine."

Roaring snowmobiles and shouts erupted outside.

"Sounds like the others are arriving," Coop said.

"Others?"

Oops. He hadn't told her. "Everybody's snowed in and without power, some with no generators to stay warm. So we decided to hold an impromptu Reclamation Committee meeting. Will you join us?"

The look of surprise on her face told him a houseful of people might not be the best way to welcome her. But there wasn't much he could do to change the weather. On the plus side, she could use some cheering up. And she'd never meet a friendlier bunch of people.

The last thing Alyssa was up for this morning was a social event. She walked into the kitchen beside Ben and settled on a stool next to Liz.

It looked as if she and the boys would be staying here, at least for now. Who knew what might change after Ben talked to his daughter?

She liked that he'd asked her to teach Hope to cook, as long as it was okay with Hope. Definitely not a sure thing, but maybe Ben would work it out with his daughter.

Clearly she wouldn't be spending a productive day organizing and cleaning as she'd planned. Instead, she'd be meeting new people. She could do that. After all, this was Ben's home. And it was up to her to go with the flow and look for ways to help out. The back door opened, closed.

"We're here," a woman's voice announced from the laundry room. Cheeks rosy, a woman who looked a lot like a chunkier version of EMT Liz walked in, followed by a heavyset man with mirth written all over him.

"Oh, look at the darling baby." The woman paused to admire Robbie, then continued her march into the kitchen. "Coop, you must have been plowing all night by the looks of the neighborhood."

"Several of us were out there having fun," Ben said. "It *is* the first snow of the season. Plowing snow next March or April? A whole different story. Alyssa, meet Lou and Harold. Lou is the force of nature I told you about. She's also

Liz's sister. And her husband Harold is the troublemaker in the group," Ben joked.

"Troublemaker?" Harold feigned chagrin. "Don't believe him for a minute."

Alyssa smiled. "Glad to meet you."

"Welcome to Rainbow Lake," Harold said.

"We met Joey outside. He's adorable." Lou stuck her hand out to shake Alyssa's firmly, then strode behind the center island, took two mugs from the cupboard and poured coffee.

Alyssa could have offered her coffee, but Lou seemed to know her way around Ben's kitchen a lot better than Alyssa did.

Harold grasped one of the coffees from his wife. "Joey and Hope are building a family of snowmen out there. I expect a visit soon for carrots and charcoal to give their family personality."

Alyssa was sure Harold's blue eyes actually twinkled.

"I hear there's a party going on." Tony's deep voice boomed from the laundry room.

"About time the Stefanos got here," EMT Max said. "We've already made all the decisions without you."

"Then we can get down to eating right away." Tony strode into the room, a large roaster in his hands.

Lou the force bustled to take the roaster from him. "Let me put that in one of Coop's fancy ovens to keep it hot. Smells like your *nonna*'s spaghetti and meatballs."

"Good nose," Tony affirmed. "Alyssa, meet my lovely wife, Maggie, and our Christmas bundle of joy." Tony beamed at the petite, very pregnant redhead as if he couldn't be prouder or more in love.

"Christmas can't come soon enough." Maggie patted her round belly. "Nice to meet you, Alyssa."

"You, too, Maggie. Your mums are beautiful." Alyssa motioned to the vase of flowers on the island.

"So glad you like them," Maggie said.

But hadn't Tony mentioned a daughter? "Is Christa outside?"

"We wish," Maggie said sadly.

Tony put his arm around his wife. "Christa lives with her adoptive mother much of the time. Thankfully, we were reunited with our daughter just last year."

Alyssa was thrilled for the couple. "What an amazing day that must have been."

"Happiest day of our lives." Giving Maggie a squeeze, Tony waved an all-encompassing hand at two people filing into the room. "My grandmother, Stella Stefano. And the last shall be first, Pastor Nick."

Smiling, Alyssa raised her hand to the twosome who also carried food. Stately Stella Stefano, the older Italian woman who had frightened her a little when she was a child. And Pastor Nick, an athletic-looking man who seemed too young to be a pastor.

Hopefully, her system to remember her father's and husband's political supporters would help her keep track of who everybody was. EMT Liz and Max; Lou the force and troublemaker Harold; pregnant Maggie and Tony; stately Stella Stefano and of course, Pastor Nick.

A few others arrived, people chatting as they drifted into Ben's living room. Alyssa asked EMT Liz to keep an eye on Robbie and ducked outside to check on Joey. Exclaiming over the snow family he and Hope were building, she was surprised how much the temperature had dropped since last night.

She hurried into the warm kitchen filled with smells of delicious, homemade cooking as Zebadiah Krentz and his old house popped into mind. "Ben, do you think Zebadiah Krentz has a generator?"

"Probably. He's been through a lot of winters here."

"I saw a phone on his counter. How can I get his number?"

"He hasn't answered his phone in years," Lou said.

"He pulled me out of the ditch last night when I slid off the road. I can't help worrying about him."

"I'll run over there and make sure he's safe." Ben strode for the laundry room. "Lou, go ahead with the meeting. I won't be long."

"I'll go." Alyssa followed him. She certainly hadn't meant to give him something else to do.

He was already putting on his jacket. "The plows probably haven't gotten to his road yet. My truck can handle it. Be right back." He hurried out the door.

She pressed her fingers to her forehead. Just in case Ben didn't have enough to do, she'd just given him something else? Of course, if Zebadiah didn't have heat, it would be worth it.

She took Robbie upstairs to feed him and put him down for his nap, then walked into the kitchen just as Ben strode in from the laundry room. "You're back."

"Stubborn old coot wouldn't come to the door. I saw his curtain move, so I know he *could* have answered."

"I didn't mean to give you another job."

"I'm glad you thought about him. But we can't help him if he won't let me in. You joining the meeting? We could use a fresh perspective."

She didn't know if she'd have anything to contribute, but she owed it to Ben to try. She walked into the living room with him.

Hope and Joey played on the computer in one corner of the room, a tired Digger sprawled at her son's feet. Everybody else lounged in a group around Lou the force writing on a pad on the couch.

"Coop, any more businesses to contribute since the mailing?" a man in the back asked.

"Afraid not." Ben grabbed a chair and offered it to Alyssa.

"Thanks," she murmured, his thoughtfulness making her feel a little self-conscious.

"Must we go back to the same people who helped us buy the building?" stately Stella asked.

"They have a stake in finishing the project, too," EMT Max asserted. "But we need a broader base. Who else can we go to?"

People shook their heads. Nobody seemed to have an answer.

"Have you checked into getting government assistance for nonprofits?" Alyssa asked tentatively.

"You mean through HUD or TIF extensions?" Tony asked.

She nodded.

Tony frowned. "I've searched high and low for help for nonprofits, but we don't meet all of the criteria. So I haven't been able to find help we qualify for."

Alyssa tried to think of possible private funding sources.

"Do you think people would get more involved if they got something for their money?" Ben asked.

Maggie frowned. "Like what?"

Again, people shook their heads with no answer.

Alyssa couldn't help being curious. "What did you do to raise funds to buy the Burkhalter Building in the first place?"

"We held several fund drives over the years, asking area churches and businesses and townsfolk to contribute to our cause," Lou the force explained. "We finally ended up with enough contributions to buy the Burkhalter Building. The problem is, we need more money to get the apartments ready to rent out."

"Have you considered doing a major fund-raiser?" Alyssa asked.

"Fund-raisers take time and are a lot of work," trouble-maker Harold chipped in.

"Yes," Alyssa agreed, "but a fund-raiser would give people who have never thought about the housing shortage the opportunity to get involved."

"That's good." Ben rubbed his jaw. "So our need is their opportunity to help."

He was definitely on the same wavelength as she was. "Isn't it?"

The group thought about it with furrowed brows.

"Problem is, I need supplies while building is slow for the winter," Tony reminded. "A fund-raiser would take time and planning we can't afford."

"Yeah," troublemaker Harold said. "If we wait too long, Tony will be back in his busy season."

"Christmas isn't far away," EMT Liz offered. "Many women don't have time to bake these days. Maybe they'd appreciate a bake sale?"

"We could throw in a silent auction along with the bake sale," Lou suggested. "I'm nearly finished with the quilt I'm working on."

"I can make some kids' toys," Max said. "The ones Sarah sells for me at her gift shop bring in more than you might imagine."

Ben looked as if he was adding the ideas up in his head and could see the money still wasn't there.

And he was right. But Alyssa had something to contribute after all: experience and insights. "These are great ideas, but they involve products that take time to make. What about adding the things you've mentioned to something bigger? Maybe a tour of the historical homes in the area?"

"I think that might appeal to people in the upscale neighborhoods," Maggie said.

"I don't know," Lou said. "Most historic homes aren't

in the best shape, and people who live in them are quite elderly. I doubt they'd feel comfortable letting strangers wander through."

"What about *one* newly restored Victorian?" Stella Stefano asked. "If Anthony and Maggie agree, I would be proud to have people tour our home."

Maggie beamed at the older woman. "That's a wonderful idea, Stella."

"It will appeal to everybody," Liz interjected. "Even people who know the Stefanos and the history of their home are probably curious to see the inside."

"What about a horse-drawn sleigh ride from town to the Stefano Victorian?" Harold ventured.

"A sleigh ride would be phenomenal," Alyssa said. "I've never been on one."

"I could go wild with Christmas decor," Maggie said. "We could sell holiday centerpieces and floral arrangements and include others in the silent auction along with Lou's quilt and Max's wooden toys."

"Don't get too carried away," Tony cautioned. "You do have to get a nursery ready before Christmas. And deliver a baby."

"That's true," Maggie admitted. "Alyssa, how soon do you think we could get a fund-raiser together? Obviously, the sooner the better for me."

"People step up planning for Christmas right after Thanksgiving," Alyssa answered. "If you get advertising out immediately, the Saturday after Thanksgiving would be perfect."

"That's less than three weeks away," somebody reminded.

"I can pull together an advertising campaign as soon as tomorrow," Ben volunteered.

People began exchanging ideas. Alyssa could feel enthusiasm building in the room, her own included.

"This project would even fit with our cause," Liz contributed. "We're reclaiming the Burkhalter Building just like the Stefanos did with the Victorian."

"All in favor of a fund-raiser at the Stefanos', say aye," Lou announced.

A hearty aye filled the room.

"Opposed?" Lou scanned the group. "Well, looks like all we need is an organizer."

Ben turned to Alyssa. "Would you consider taking this on?"

"Me?" she sputtered. She glanced at the animated faces around her and felt more alive than she had for a long while. "But I'm not a member of your committee."

"Then we'll appoint you one." Ben grinned. "We really need your help."

Hadn't she been looking for a way she could repay him for everything? Besides, she'd been doing whatever she could to help low-income families for as long as she could remember. She'd also excelled at working on her father's and Cam's fund-raisers. So not only was this in her ballpark, but she also had the know-how to hit the ball clear out of the park.

But she had to be realistic. There were only so many hours in a day, and she had a lot to get done before her parents arrived for Christmas. "I'm just not sure I'll have time. I need to care for the boys and find a job."

"We desperately need an office manager and all-around organizer at the church," Pastor Nick said. "The council has approved the position, but we haven't found anybody to fill it. If the Reclamation fund-raiser was your first project to organize, would you be interested in the job, Alyssa?"

Her mouth flew open before she could stop it. Pastor Nick was offering her a job at the church? But church people were big on charity. At least, they had been in Madison. Was that why the pastor was being so generous? Had Ben told him about Cam, and that she needed to support her boys? She shot a look at Ben.

He gave her an encouraging smile.

"You could work at home some days," Pastor Nick said. "We have a day-care center, too, for days you need to work at church."

Working at home part of the week sounded ideal. And she could certainly use the money. Alyssa looked at the supportive expressions on Ben's friends' faces. No question, organizing the fund-raiser would be a great use of her talents, plus she'd be helping Ben work for his cause.

But if the job was an act of charity, she'd be right back where she started. "I'm sorry but I can't accept."

Pastor Nick looked puzzled. "I'm sure we can't offer you what you're worth, but maybe we can work out a compromise. Please take your time to think about it. If you have questions, you can give me a call."

She sighed, effectively agreeing to think about it. But only because she needed to find out if Ben and the pastor had decided to make her the church's new project.

Chapter Six

With the boys tucked in and Hope reading in the living room cuddled beside Digger, Alyssa poured a cup of tea from the electric teapot she'd dug out of her things. She needed to talk to Ben about Pastor Nick's job offer. "Would you like cinnamon tea?"

"It smells terrific, but no thanks." Standing at the island counter, he clicked a few keys on his laptop, then stepped back and offered her the stool. "I'll show you the plans for the Burkhalter Building."

Tea in hand, she decided to put off her questions for the moment. Settling on the stool, she studied the computer screen.

He moved behind her to look over her shoulder, his fresh outdoors scent mingling with the cinnamon.

Nice combination. "I see two two-bedroom units on the first floor and one on the second? Is there a laundry?"

"There's a Laundromat next door."

"It will cost the renters extra for laundry that way."

He pointed to the plans. "We planned a large-enough bathroom to allow for stackable machines right here if we end up having enough money for them."

"That's smart." She pointed at the screen. "I like the balcony upstairs."

"I've lived in enough upstairs apartments to know how claustrophobic they can get without access to the outside." His warm breath ruffled her hair.

A little shiver tweaked her nerves. She dismissed it. "How long do you think it will take to get the building ready for occupancy once you have money to go ahead?"

"Tony promises a couple months. We've already gutted and cleaned out the building, even ripped down these walls." He pointed out the ones he meant, his arm brushing her shoulder as he leaned in.

She swallowed, doing her best to ignore his closeness. Stillness hovered between them for a moment.

He pulled back and moved to sit on the stool beside her. "So there you have it."

She let out a breath, took a sip of tea, attempted to refocus on the plans. "These are very impressive."

"I'd rather show you the real project, but this will do for now."

"You're really invested in this, aren't you?"

"You saw that there's no housing out there. Hope and I had to live in a motor home on the property while I cleared the land and Tony helped me build the house. But back to the Burkhalter Building. You seemed to have really got into planning the fund-raiser."

She had. The idea still intrigued her, but… "What can I say? Fund-raisers are part of my DNA."

"I don't know if we can pull it off unless you organize it."

She gave him a pained look. "Of course you can. You have a talented group there."

"We do, but nobody has experience working on such an ambitious fund-raiser as this one. I'm glad Pastor Nick realized you could help and offered you a job. I'm surprised you didn't accept it on the spot."

She wouldn't get a better chance to ask her question. "Did you talk to the pastor about giving me a job?"

"No. Why?"

She nibbled her lip, trying to decide if she believed him. She did. "Just being paranoid, I guess. I didn't come to Rainbow Lake to have people take care of me."

"Got that memo." He gave her a questioning look. "Can't say I understand why you're so concerned about accepting help when you need it, though."

"I've relied on my parents too much my entire life. And I relied too much on Cam, as well. When he died—" She pressed her hand to her forehead to stop emotions she didn't want to feel.

Ben looked at her as if he empathized with her pain. "It had to be a terrible shock not only to lose your husband, but also to suddenly be alone with a little boy and a baby on the way. How did you manage to get through it?"

A chill shook her. "I didn't," she whispered.

"You didn't? What do you mean?"

"I couldn't…do it." She shook her head and did her best to shut down the building nausea.

He peered at her intently. "What happened?"

She didn't have an answer to his question, at least, not one that would ever satisfy her. "I folded up in a heap. Disappeared really…in every way that counted." She blew out a breath. "I completely abandoned my son when he lost his daddy." She shook her head, desperately wanting to deny that knowledge.

Ben's expression encouraged her to go on.

"I only know that after the policewoman left, I was bathing Joey before I put him to bed. But—" She shook her head, doing her best to think through what had happened for the billionth time. "I couldn't get him out of the tub. I couldn't move, couldn't think. I was too weak and helpless to take care of my child. Or myself."

"Alyssa—" Ben grasped her hand "—it's okay."

"It will never be okay." But she had to get hold of herself. Squeezing her eyes closed, she concentrated on facing the pain the way her therapist had taught her. Slowly, slowly... the nausea faded. "I'm sorry."

"Don't be. You should have had somebody with you. It sounds like you were in shock."

"My grief therapist said it was my body's way of protecting itself and the baby I was carrying."

"Pretty miraculous, don't you think?"

She nodded. "But being overwhelmed and helpless is terrifying. I'll do anything never to experience that again."

"My dad used to tell me that my weakness pointed to God's strength."

She lifted her hands to her hot cheeks. "I'm not following."

"My mother left my dad and me when I was eight. I couldn't eat, couldn't sleep. My dad told me to lay my weakness at Jesus's feet and ask Him to fill me. The best advice he ever gave me."

"So you did?"

"I did. Still do."

She sighed. "I don't know if I can do that, but I'll try. Thank you for sharing that with me. I'm really sorry your mother left when you were a child."

"Thanks. But you were telling me what happened when your husband died. Did your parents come to Madison when you needed them?"

She took a shaky breath. "They arranged everything. The funeral, the burial. Mother even put her life on hold and lived with us for a month. When she had to go back, she and Daddy insisted we move to Washington to live with them."

"Did you?"

"I couldn't leave our home. I just couldn't."

"What happened?"

"The wonderful grief therapist Mother had found for me advised my parents against uprooting us from our home so soon after Cam's death." She sighed. "So Mother enlisted friends and people from the church to take care of us." She took a deep breath. "I was on bed rest for months with Robbie, and those wonderful people took care of us. I was completely useless. To Joey. Even to myself."

He gave her a glimpse of a smile. "Not to the baby you were carrying. God took good care of you and your boys," he said softly.

"Yes," she agreed. "But I came to Rainbow Lake to learn to take care of myself. Like Gram did."

"Then the job fits right in with your plan, doesn't it?"

"It does. But I've been on the receiving end long enough."

"You're not on the receiving end this time."

"What do you mean?"

"You're more than qualified for the job, Alyssa. The church is fortunate to get you."

Did he mean it? Or was he just telling her that to make her feel better?

"You know one of the things I like most about the church?"

"What's that?" she asked cautiously.

"It's not only a place to receive help, but it's also an excellent place to give back."

"Give back? I like *that* idea." She remembered the way people had treated her at the meeting. They hadn't looked at her with sympathy…like she needed help, had they? They'd respected her input. They'd even asked her to chair their fund-raiser. They wouldn't have done that out of pity, right? Hadn't they asked her to be part of their group as an equal contributor to their cause? She smiled.

"I like your smile. I'd like to see more of it."

Suddenly self-conscious, she looked at the floor. She'd told him things in the past few minutes she'd told only her therapist and a few people she trusted. She'd learned early to keep her thoughts to herself or risk embarrassing her senator father. But apparently, she completely trusted Ben. And he was so easy to talk to. She hoped he didn't mind.

"So you're thinking you'll take the job?" he asked.

She was. It seemed perfect. There was only one hurdle she could think of. "Before I can accept it, I need to check out the day-care center."

"Right." He was quiet for a couple beats. "I'll meet you at church tomorrow. I can show you around, and we'll look at the child-care center and see what you think."

A flutter of relief wound through her. Going to the church wouldn't be easy. She hadn't been able to go to church since Cam's funeral. Having Ben with her would help. She wouldn't have to go alone, but— "You have to work."

"That's one of the perks of owning the newspaper. I can take a lunch break whenever I want to."

After checking out the day-care center the next morning and getting Joey and sleeping Robbie safely deposited for a short trial, Coop clasped Alyssa's elbow and quickly escorted her out of the room before she could change her mind about leaving them. Wanting to show her around the church, he walked up the hall beside her, feeling more protective than ever because she'd entrusted him with her fears yesterday evening.

Her openness amazed and humbled him. He'd known she'd been through a lot over the past year, but he'd had no clue how much she'd suffered. He had only respect for her. *Only respect, Coop? You sure that's all you feel?*

"Three teachers for thirteen children seems like a very good ratio," she said. "I like that they use a video to hold the kids' interest in storytelling, too. And what could be more perfect than a child-care guy who loves superheroes? He even knelt to Joey's level to interact with him."

"Any red flags?"

"I can't think of any. Not with the center. Only with my comfort level in leaving them. I'm beginning to think *I'm* the one with separation anxiety."

"We're working on that."

She smiled. "Yes, we are."

He loved her smile; it made him feel like everything was okay. "We are now entering the Sunday school wing." He gave her a quick tour. They peeked in the door of the nursery for rambunctious kids during church services and viewed the large fellowship room. Then he took her to his favorite part—the sanctuary.

Sun refracted rich colors through the stained-glass windows like a kaleidoscope, the empty sanctuary still and peaceful, yet filled with a sense of anticipation.

Alyssa glanced around at the vibrant colors and rich woods, but it was the large, wooden cross over the altar that caught her attention and held it. "It's beautiful," she said in a hushed voice.

He turned to her.

She stood there, looking up at the cross, her lovely face bathed in tears.

His throat felt thick. Maybe he shouldn't have brought her here. Hadn't she said she hadn't been to church in a while? Hurting for her, he handed her his handkerchief.

She accepted it and dabbed at her tears. "I'm sorry. Whenever I think I'm moving past that awful time, something catches me by surprise and I'm right back there. His death. That horrible helpless feeling. That was the worst of all."

"The last time you were in church was for your husband's funeral?"

She nodded.

"I'm sorry." He grasped her hand and guided her down the aisle, stopping in the entry hall. "I brought you here too soon."

"No, you're helping me face my fears. That's a good thing."

"It's been only a year, hasn't it?"

"It will be…a couple days after Thanksgiving."

A couple days— "The fund-raiser will be two days after Thanksgiving. Is that why you hesitated about planning it? Why didn't you tell me? We'd all understand, Alyssa."

"That's not the reason I hesitated about the job. And I don't want everybody's understanding. I want to give back. And having a purpose that day will help."

He swallowed around a lump in his throat. "Spoken like a strong woman."

"*Strong* woman?" She threw him a questioning look.

"Absolutely."

"I'm *not* strong. Far from it."

She was stronger than she knew. But the pain in her voice touched him deeply, made him want to make everything better for her—everything.

He looked into her blue, blue eyes, an unfamiliar stillness filling him. Protecting her and her boys was only part of it. The other part…the exciting, terrifying part was that he wanted to take care of *her* with an intensity he'd never before experienced.

How could it be possible to have such strong feelings for her in a matter of days? No question in his mind, he wanted more than friendship with her.

When had that happened? Where was he planning on going with this? What about risking Hope? What about the fact that Alyssa was still grieving her husband? Not the best timing, Coop.

Is this Your doing, God? Did You bring this beautiful, amazing woman and her boys here to become an important part of our lives? Or is she here only to test my commitment to keep Hope safe?

How was he going to figure it all out? And just how much was he willing to risk to try?

Ben went back to the newspaper, and Alyssa worked through the practicalities of the job with Pastor Nick. Now, she followed the pastor down the hall to look at her office next door to his, her thoughts wandering back to Ben. He seemed to take in stride her reluctance to be in a church since Cam's funeral. He'd actually called her strong for facing her fears. He seemed to know exactly what to say to make her feel good about herself.

"The room's small but adequate, I think." Pastor Nick opened the door into a room filled with natural light pouring through the large window that looked out on snow-laden trees in the yard facing Main Street.

She scanned the partially filled bookshelves lining the wall behind the wonderful old, oak desk that dominated the space. "This is a pleasant little room," she said sincerely.

He smiled. "Can you see yourself working here a few hours a week? Though I'm sure you can do most of the work at home near your children."

"Sounds wonderful. Yes, I can imagine myself working here some days."

"Good. How's your cottage coming along?"

"Tony and his men cleaned it out this morning. Every-thing in the living room was either worn-out or ruined by smoke or water, so I need to figure out what I'll do for furniture on my limited budget."

"There are several shops you might want to check out. Ask Lou which ones. She knows everything about this town."

"Thanks, I'll do that."

"I want to thank you for looking out for Zebadiah Krentz during the blizzard."

"He lives in pretty primitive conditions."

"I stop there occasionally, but he always refuses to open the door for me. I'm thankful he did for you."

"He knew my father and my grandparents. That seemed to be the key."

"You know, some people, even when they desperately need help, feel it's demeaning to ask for it." He gave her a meaningful look. "They'd rather go without than need someone."

Ignoring his gaze, she looked at her watch. "I have to leave. Joey needs a nap before we go on Harold's sleigh ride later. He's really looking forward to it."

"I am, too. Aren't you?"

She nodded.

"I hope you'll build on your contact with Zebadiah. I have a feeling he's one of those people I'm talking about."

Alyssa took a step back, relieved he didn't seem to be talking about her. But he was giving her the chance to be the helper instead of being the helped? "What do you think he needs?"

"A friend. He doesn't seem to know it, but I think that's it. I hope you'll be his friend."

"I'm just not sure I'd make a good friend right now."

"Ben mentioned your husband was killed this past year. Actually, I'm impressed with how well you're doing."

"You are?"

"Very. I'm sure it hasn't been easy, but moving here was a big step. It takes some people years to move on after losing a loved one. Some are never able to do it. I believe you're just what Zebadiah needs."

"You really think I can help?"

He nodded.

"Then I'll do my best."

He smiled. "I'm sure you can reach him in a way I can't. Thank you, Alyssa."

"I hope I don't disappoint you."

"I'm not the least concerned about that. Don't you be concerned either. Just do what you can."

Friendships weren't always built in a few days. Not like hers and Ben's had been. Come to think of it, she'd never become friends with anybody so quickly, let alone so easily spilling her problems and secrets. Then again, how many people had she met like Ben Cooper?

She gathered her things and headed down the hall to the day care to get the boys. Walking past the closed doors of the sanctuary on the way, she remembered the pain that had ripped through her earlier. Pain as fresh as the night the policewoman had rapped on her door when Cam hadn't come home from a quick run to the convenience store. Remembered struggling with nausea and focusing on her pain until it subsided. Remembered Ben escorting her out of the sanctuary.

She stopped, made herself open the door and walk in. The cross commanded her attention the way it had before. But this time, there was less pain, little nausea. No tears. Only thoughts of Ben and her new job and befriending Zebadiah Krentz spun in her mind.

She was facing Cam's death. And she was moving ahead with her life. It felt really good to be on the giving end for a change.

Chapter Seven

The rich smells of leather and horses mingled with the fresh scents of snow and the straw padding the sleigh box. Coop watched Harold drive his team of prancing, snorting draft horses along the county road. Hope rode shotgun, thanks to Harold always treating her like one of his granddaughters.

The sleighful of friends and relatives talked and laughed, everybody excited that Alyssa had accepted the job at church and would be organizing the fund-raiser. Sandwiched between Pastor Nick and Alyssa with Robbie in her arms, Coop held Joey close to keep him steady.

The little guy's eyes were fastened on the big, bobbing heads of the horses. He'd wanted to bring Digger along, but Coop convinced him there wasn't room for a ninety-pound dog, especially one who barked at anything that moved.

Alyssa's eyes were almost as wide as Joey's. Coop couldn't seem to keep from watching her.

"Isn't this exciting, Joey?" Alyssa beamed at her son.

She always had a smile for her boys. He liked that about her. *Face it, Coop. What don't you like about her?*

Leaving her at the church this morning had been difficult. He'd wanted to stay for moral support if nothing else, but she'd insisted he go back to the paper instead. "You doing okay?" he asked quietly.

"I'm doing great. What about you?"

"Fine." Truth was, he'd be doing a whole lot better if he hadn't realized how he felt about her.

Harold turned the team onto a small road into his hayfield, people laughing and scrambling to hang on during the turn.

Coop grasped the side of the sleigh and held Joey tighter to keep him upright. In the slippery cushion of straw, he slid into Nick, the soft bump of Alyssa's hip an unexpected pleasure. He turned to her. "Gotta watch those turns."

Her pretty pink flush told him she was probably embarrassed.

He held her gaze, looking for what, he couldn't be sure.

A tiny smile crinkled the corners of her eyes.

He smiled in return.

She dropped her gaze, but she didn't move away.

That special stillness filled him just as it had in the sanctuary. Did she feel it, too? Did he dare hope for that? Or was he out on this limb all by himself?

The horses strained to slog through huge snowdrifts the wind had banked in the open field, the sleigh bouncing and jerking with their efforts.

Coop simply enjoyed Alyssa's closeness and did his best to ignore the caution sign blinking in his mind's eye. So he wanted to be close to the pretty woman beside him. It didn't mean he planned to do anything about it, right?

Joey turned to him with a serious look. "The black horse is named Jack. That lady told me." He pointed to Lou. "And the white horse is Dolly." The boy leaned closer and cupped his hand to whisper loudly in Coop's ear. "I like Jack best, but I don't want to hurt Dolly's feelings."

Coop tugged the kid's hat to allow him to see better.

"That's very considerate, Joey," Nick commented.

Joey eyed the pastor. "I don't know that word," he said shyly.

Nick was obviously surprised. He always seemed a little mystified by young kids.

"Considerate means you think about others," Coop offered.

"That's right." Nick gave Coop a lifted eyebrow. "Thanks."

Coop grinned. "It helps to have a kid of your own."

Nick chuckled. "Someday, I hope. Until then, I'll use you as a resource."

"Feel free."

Jostling her baby, Alyssa struggled to maintain her balance.

"Lean on me." Coop turned his back to her.

"Thanks." She positioned herself to take advantage of his support.

He liked that she'd taken him up on his offer without hesitation. Made him feel good…like anything could be possible.

But before long, the sleigh broke free with a bone-jostling shudder, its runners skimming through smooth snow on a firm snowmobile trail kept void of drifts by the dense forest of firs shielding it. Unfortunately, Alyssa moved away a little.

He missed her warmth.

"Sorry about that rough patch," Harold tossed back to his passengers. "The ride will be smooth as glass from here."

"Thanks to the Noah's Crossing Snowmobilers' Club for planting rows of trees a few years back to block drifting," Max bragged.

Harold raised his arm in acknowledgment. A man of his word, he guided the team through the hushed winter wonderland, the thud of horses' hooves in the snow as steady as the beat of Coop's heart.

Joey cupped his hand around Coop's ear again.

Coop leaned closer.

"Can I sit by the horses with Hope?" the kid asked in a loud whisper that included plenty of spit.

"Harold, is there room for Joey to sit with you and Hope for a while?"

"Sure thing. Hand him up. Hope's doing a fine job driving the horses."

Hope flashed a victory smile over her shoulder.

"Will you hang on very, very tight?" Alyssa asked.

Joey gave her a serious nod.

"Okay, then." Alyssa looked squarely at Coop, making it clear she was trusting him on this.

Feeling great to have her trust him with something so important as her son's welfare, Coop lifted Joey to Max. "Boy coming through."

"Got him." Max turned and planted Joey firmly in Harold's waiting arms.

Coop settled back to enjoy the scenery. Tall firs layered with snow softened the landscape. A pair of cardinals, the male brilliant against the snow-covered pines, flitted through the trees. The birds called to each other in soft, staccato chirps like surveyors mapping new terrain now that the snow had blurred familiar landmarks.

Coop silently pointed at a doe and fawn standing as still as statues as the mother sniffed the air for danger.

With the baby dozing in her arms, Alyssa leaned against the side of the sleigh box, her deep blue eyes watching the doe reach for a low branch of a cedar. "That looks like the chapel where my gram and gramps were married." She pointed.

He peered through the trees, the small stone building topped with a white steeple standing out in the sea of white. "It's the old community church."

"Harold's ancestors donated the land," Lou said, "and farmers in the area built the church, Liz and my ancestors included."

"Gram took me there once. I'm so happy to see it again!" Alyssa exclaimed.

Coop couldn't help smiling at the excitement in her voice. Amazing how much her happiness affected him. And when it came right down to it, he couldn't change the way she made him feel. But why would he want to when it was so good?

Wait a minute.

Protecting Hope was the most important thing he'd ever taken on. Did he really have to remind himself how badly he'd let her down when he'd trusted Denise to care for her? When he'd fired the caretaker, Hope had been devastated. How much worse would it be if he invited a woman into their personal lives and the relationship ended for some reason?

He'd not pursued a serious relationship since he had Hope. He'd never seemed to have time. And honestly, he hadn't met anybody he wanted to pursue. Why now? Hope would be going off to college in a few short years. Maybe he'd fill that part of his life then. Who knew?

He studied Alyssa's profile, a smile tweaking his lips. She was the answer to *Why now?*

And as to what he was going to do about his feelings for her? All he could do was figure it out as he went. And pray. *Dear God, give me the perspective to see how my feelings for Alyssa could affect not only Hope but Alyssa and her boys. And give me the wisdom to figure out what's best for all of us.*

Breaking free of the protection of trees, Harold turned the team onto the county road toward home. Everybody scrambled for balance again.

Alyssa decided the delicious casserole Tony's grand-mother sent over after the fire was the perfect dinner solution that evening. Cleaning up the kitchen afterward, Hope asked her dad to take her and Joey sledding on Walnut Hill. Being the great dad he was, Ben agreed to put off the article he needed to write for the paper until later and take them all to Walnut Hill.

Now, Alyssa cuddled Robbie on the summit, the full moon bathing the snow-softened hillside and highlighting clusters of families or teenagers sliding down or climbing up the hill. The air was crisp as Ben pulled Joey up the hill on the toboggan, Hope walking alongside.

When they arrived, he'd insisted on holding Robbie to allow Alyssa to take a few rides down the hill with Hope and Joey. Surprisingly, Robbie had thought Ben holding him was just fine. It looked as if her baby had gotten used to having Ben around. She wished he'd accept Hope, too.

Hope soon let Alyssa know she would rather be sledding with her dad, and who could blame her? She was used to having her dad all to herself. Determined to avoid anything that might complicate the wonderful relationship Ben had with his daughter, Alyssa insisted he take his turn. And so he did.

Now, she watched him line up the toboggan on the crest of the hill and thought about how much she'd enjoyed sitting with him on the sleigh ride this afternoon. She hadn't realized how much she missed the warmth of being close with a man. Or his occasional unexpected touch or smile. But then, Ben wasn't just any man.

She watched him give the kids a shove, turn and stride toward her. She did her best to tamp down her skittish pulse. "Having fun?"

"Yeah." He gave her his secret-weapon smile. "You?"

"Yes." *Of course,* she smiled in return. It was impossible not to. "I've never been on Walnut Hill before. I was here only for summers, you know."

"You think you'll stay at Rainbow Lake for a while?"

"As long as I can."

"Indefinitely, maybe?"

"Maybe. I love it here."

"I sure understand that."

"You said you've been here for seven years. I'm surprised you haven't gotten married and settled down with somebody by now." Did she sound as if she was fishing for information? She hoped not. She wasn't, was she? "Just curious," she qualified.

"Matchmaking around here is pretty much a spectator sport."

She shook her head, not understanding. "Spectator sport?"

"Dates in Chicago used to be casual, fun, no big deal. Here, they're a news event that invites the whole town to forecast the future of the pair. Not a bad thing if you're hoping for a future with the woman in question. Otherwise, you don't date."

"You're exaggerating."

"Unfortunately, no. At least, not by much. Between that and never having the time, I haven't ventured into dating for a long time."

"Sounds awful."

"Yeah. I suppose if I'd found the right woman—" he kicked at the snow with his boot "—then maybe it would be worth taking a chance?"

"You're asking *me* that question?"

Nodding, he peered at her as if her answer was important.

Confusion muddled her. "Are you asking me for dating advice?"

"Just wondering what you think about taking a chance on the right person."

She nibbled her lip. Tried to give his question the thought

it deserved, then sighed. "I've never been much of a risk taker. I think life is enough of a risk to begin with."

"I can see how you might feel that way, especially given your situation." He looked glum. "Me? I've always been concerned about risking Hope's sense of security."

"By a woman rejecting her, you mean?"

"Yeah. Or being insensitive to her or unable to love her. I don't know. It's something I worry about."

"Then you're not thinking about dating the right kind of woman." The problem was, she didn't want to think about him being involved with any woman. Any woman other than herself? But that was crazy.

He raised an eyebrow. "Which kind of woman would that be?"

"Any woman who wouldn't have your family's best interest at heart."

He studied her intently, then nodded. "Good point."

Hope and Joey reached the top of the hill.

"Come on, Dad. Go down with us this time."

"Still catching my breath, kiddo."

Hope glowered at Alyssa.

"She really wants you to go with her. Please don't let me stop you," Alyssa said quietly.

"You guys go ahead. I'll go with you next time."

"Hang on, Joey. You ready?"

"Ready."

Hope pushed off, and they went streaking down the hill. Ben turned to Alyssa.

After their serious conversation on dating, Alyssa was ready to lighten the mood. She focused on the Chicago Bears emblem on Ben's headband. "There's something I don't understand."

"What's that?"

"How do you get away with supporting the Bears in Green Bay Packers territory?"

"Not easily. I get in some pretty heated conversations. Max and Harold accuse me of being a traitor. But my dad and I cheered for the Bears long before I knew Max and Harold, so they've conceded I'm a lost cause. You like football?"

"I don't know anything about it."

"I guess I figured that out when you took off to look for rentals Sunday afternoon instead of watching the game."

"Maybe you can teach me a few things about it?"

"You're on."

Robbie gave her a toothless smile.

She smiled back. "Robbie seems to have accepted you."

"He watched me pretty closely."

"But he cries for everybody else."

"I'm glad he didn't do that. Tears get me every time."

"Uh-oh. Is that why you invited me to stay in your guest room the night of the fire? To stop my tears?"

"Probably." He met her gaze, mischief in his eyes. "Honestly? I don't remember why I invited you to stay."

"Because you, Ben Cooper, like taking care of people."

"Do I?"

"Especially kids. And dogs. Hope told us you rescued Digger after a car hit him."

"I'm gaining more than I gave, don't you think?"

She nodded. "Unlike with me."

"Not true. Don't think I haven't noticed you've been cleaning and tidying up the place. And I could get used to having you and the boys live with us just for your cooking."

She gave him a little smile. "Better be careful. Maybe *we'll* stay forever." Oh, that didn't sound right. "I mean, like Digger."

"Okay. Stay forever."

She laughed nervously. "Nice save."

The kids reached the top of the hill again.

"See ya." Ben strode to keep the promise he'd made to his daughter.

After working at the church for a few hours the next morning, Alyssa made a quick stop for groceries. Then she bought a cell at the phone store and walked out, holding Robbie and clasping Joey's hand. The *Courier* marquee across the street snagged her attention. "Look, Joey. That's where Ben works."

"Can we go see him?"

He'd still been working in his home office last night when she'd gone up to bed. She'd never been in a small-town newspaper office. Did Ben have employees or did he do everything himself?

"Can we, Mommy?"

Why not? The thought of seeing him made her as happy as her son. Besides, she was curious to see where he worked. And maybe if he had time, he'd mentioned he wanted to show her the Burkhalter Building. "Shall we surprise him?"

Joey did an excited little hop, haphazardly juggling the phone bag she'd given him to carry.

She stashed the package in the car, then walked toward the newspaper office, Joey at her side. She opened the door and entered the noisy, bustling office she hadn't expected.

"Where's Ben, Mommy?" Joey sounded worried.

He was probably busy. She shouldn't have come. At least, not without calling. She turned to leave.

But the pretty, young woman behind the reception desk had stopped typing and had already snatched her earphones off her head. "What can I do for you?"

Alyssa stepped closer to her desk. "We're looking for Ben Cooper."

"I'm sorry. Mr. Cooper isn't available. Can I help?"

"I didn't realize—"

"Clint, where's the background article on the Burkhalter Building?" Ben's rich bass cut through the din.

"Ben!" Joey pulled his hand from Alyssa's grasp and charged through the flurry of activity.

"Hey, Joey." Ben swooped the boy up into his arms. He wore khakis and a blue oxford button-down shirt, sleeves rolled up. Very professional-and-polished-looking. Knowing Ben, she wouldn't expect anything less.

"Are you surprised?" Joey asked.

"Very. Where's your—" He gave Alyssa a welcoming smile as if he was glad to see her. "Here she is."

Alyssa smiled back, if a little chagrined. "I didn't realize how busy you'd be today."

"It's always like this. I'd like to give you a tour, but we'll wait until sometime when we're closed." He glanced around.

People who'd stopped to watch the interchange quickly got back to work. Alyssa felt very conspicuous. "We'll just get out of your hair."

"I want to find out how your first day on the job went. And while you're in town, I'll show you the Burkhalter Building. Just let me get my jacket." With Joey in his arms, Ben hurried away, issuing changes he wanted in a layout as he went.

She walked back to the front of the office to wait near the door, noting the young woman behind the reception desk was transcribing again.

Ben soon strode through the bustling room with Joey riding his shoulders, stopping to answer questions and make decisions on the way.

He commanded his office much the way Cam and her father did, making decisions without hesitating. Funny, she hadn't thought about the men being similar.

Of course, they were different in many ways, too.

Walking toward her, Ben gave her one of his disarming smiles.

The only thing she could do was answer his smile with one of her own.

He opened the door for her, then followed her outside, ducking to make sure Joey didn't bump his head. Grasping her elbow, he walked beside her. "Thanks for stopping to see me. What a thoughtful thing to do."

Leave it to Ben to try to convince her that she hadn't thrown a wrench in his workday. "I would have called to see if you had time, but I had no idea you worked in such a hectic place. How in the world do you find so much news to report in such a small town?"

He laughed. "The *Courier* covers news in the Noah's Crossing area. But we also supplement and print an area trade paper and village newspapers for three nearby towns. Keeps us hopping and then some."

"Sounds like pressure to me."

"We have a lot of deadlines to meet. People want to know what's going on in their towns."

"It doesn't seem that different from a city newspaper."

"It's not all that different. All good newspapers bring problems into focus so they can be fixed. How did the boys do at the day-care center?"

"We made amimal cookies," Joey reported. "And Brett and Trent and me were superheroes, and we played Chutes and Ladders and Trent helped me make four puzzles 'cause he's four, too. And Matt read a book with little pitures for us to read. Robbie cried, but Mrs. Roxanne sang to him, and he stopped crying so he could hear her."

So that was how Mrs. Roxanne had won Robbie over. Alyssa smiled at Joey's enthusiasm. "There's your answer."

"Good job, Joey and Robbie," Ben encouraged. "How did it go for you?" He gave her a concerned look.

"Almost as great."

"You felt comfortable there?"

She nodded. "I did."

He looked relieved. "Great. Ah, here we are…future home of low-income family housing." He unlocked the door and let her inside. "Sorry, it's not very warm. We heat it just enough to keep pipes from freezing." With Joey still riding his shoulders, Ben gave her a tour of the mostly open space, explaining the planned layout as they went.

"It will be very nice. Are you including a picture or two of the committee's progress in the *Courier* along with news about the fund-raiser?"

"Not sure pictures of a big empty space will show much."

"It will show why the committee's holding a fund-raiser, and give people who donated to help purchase the building a feeling of ownership."

He nodded. "Good point. I'll look through pictures I've taken through the process. I should have a few good ones."

"Before and after, maybe?"

He grinned. "I should have hired you to work at the newspaper."

"I'm impressed with the progress the committee's made, and I'm sure other people will be, too."

"Thanks for your advice."

"It's the least I can do."

He gave his head a little shake. "You don't need to repay me."

"I enjoy doing things to thank you," she said honestly.

His rugged face melted in a warm smile. "Perfect answer, pretty lady."

Absorbing the effects of his smile, she gave him a saucy look. "Seeing that charm of yours peek through is my reward."

"Charm?"

"It works for me." What was she doing? Trying to flirt? She never flirted. She'd always been terrible at it. But it had happened so naturally with him that she hadn't realized she was doing it.

"Really. Then I should use my charm more often?" He looked amused with just the right touch of seriously wanting an answer to his question.

Nicely done. All she could do was smile, noting that he seemed to enjoy the banter as much as she did.

Chapter Eight

Driving home that evening, Coop thought about Alyssa's surprise visit. That she'd thought about stopping in made him smile. She and her boys had created quite a stir.

When he'd returned from showing her the Burkhalter Building, a colleague had commented that everybody was shocked when Coop left in the middle of pressing deadlines. Funny, he hadn't given deadlines a second thought. Not his normal behavior for sure.

He pulled into his drive, killed the motor and jumped out of his truck. Striding for the back door, he realized he hadn't spent his short drive home working out problems and setting goals for the next day the way he usually did. Instead, he'd been thinking about Alyssa's visit, about her waiting at home. Shaking his head, he pulled open the door and shut it behind him, wonderful Italian smells coming from the kitchen.

"Hi, Ben. I'm feeding Digger."

Digger danced between Coop and the food Joey scooped into the dish, poor dog torn between two loves.

Giving Dig a quick scratch behind his ears, Coop smiled at Joey's earnest face. "Looks like you're doing a great job." He shrugged off his jacket. "Just one scoop, right?"

Joey nodded. "Hope showed me how."

"Great." He hung his jacket on a peg.

"Hope, it's easier and safer to use the colander to drain spaghetti and many things you boil," Alyssa's gentle voice directed.

Must be a cooking lesson going on. He walked into the kitchen, his gaze zooming to Alyssa working at the counter in slim, dark jeans and a soft pink sweater that gave her fair skin a healthy glow. His breath hitched.

Spinning greens in a gadget he'd never seen before, Alyssa gave him a little smile. "Did you put the newspaper to bed?"

"Sure did." Beaming from the inside out, he got lost in her deep blue gaze. "Thanks for stopping to see me today."

"We enjoyed it, too." She glanced at Hope.

He turned his focus on Robbie cooing at his wrist rattle in his carrier on the island. Joey's cars lay scattered near him. What a wonderful scene to come home to. An amazing woman, children's toys and aromas of delicious food cooking. "Smells great in here."

"We're having spaghetti and meatballs." Hope looked up from her task, steam rising around her.

"Careful," Alyssa reminded.

"I *have* cooked before, you know," Hope said abruptly.

Coop scowled at the back of his daughter's head. Apparently, things weren't going as well as he'd thought.

"Hope, will you please turn down the heat under the sauce and stir it to keep it from scorching?" Alyssa asked.

Hope set the spaghetti pot on the stove with a thud and turned down the burner under the sauce before she grabbed the wooden spoon and began stirring.

She was following Alyssa's directions, but her body language told Coop his daughter wasn't happy. He realized that with everything going on, he still hadn't had that talk with her that he'd promised Alyssa he would. He'd better get it done soon.

"My meatball broke." Joey's mouth drew into a pout.

Coop ruffled his hair. "Your hands have to grow a bit, that's all. Then you'll make great meatballs."

Seeming satisfied with that explanation, Joey climbed onto a stool to play with his cars.

Alyssa tore romaine and endive she took from the spinning gadget into a glass bowl she must have dug out of the things they'd carried to his basement to allow her to return her rental U-Haul. "Hope, make sure you dip the spoon all the way to the bottom. You need to stir the sauce closest to the heat."

Hope gave Alyssa an exasperated look.

"Here, I'll show you." Alyssa moved closer, took the spoon from Hope and demonstrated what she meant.

"Whatever you say," Hope snapped.

"Hope, Alyssa is being kind enough to show you how to cook—"

"My cooking's been fine until she moved in."

He frowned, surprised by her retort. It just wasn't like her.

"Hope," Alyssa said, "I had to take a basic cooking class after I got married because I didn't know a thing about it. But you already know so much. I'm only showing you the finer points to help you improve."

Hope looked at Alyssa, as if trying to decide if she could trust her words.

Holding the girl's gaze, Alyssa raised her hand, swearing to the truth.

Hope turned back to the sauce. Alyssa relinquished the spoon, and Hope took over the stirring. "Is this right?"

"Perfect." Alyssa went back to fixing the salad.

Alyssa knew how to calm Hope, but his daughter had been known to carry a grudge. Add the fact that she seemed to be turning into a woman way too fast, with all the wonders and complexities he would never understand, and he could have reason to worry. Obviously, he needed to have that talk with her right after supper.

When all were seated around the table, Coop said grace, Hope served the spaghetti and meatballs while Alyssa passed filled salad bowls. Finally, everybody dug in.

"We went to see Mr. Krentz today," Joey announced.

"He opened the door?" Coop asked.

"I don't think he wanted to," Alyssa said. "I asked him if he had a generator. He does, but it was on the fritz in this last storm, so he slept on the kitchen floor near his woodstove. I tried to persuade him to let you take a look at it, which only made him grumpier. We didn't stay long."

"Can't help him if he doesn't want it," Coop said. "I talked to Tony this afternoon. He mentioned you'd been taking measurements at the cottage while the boys were napping."

"I need to look for furniture that will fit. I was surprised at how much work they've already done. Tony says they're right on schedule."

The meal ended with rave reviews, and Coop began clearing the table. "How about helping me with kitchen cleanup, Hope? We need to talk."

Alyssa eyed Coop. "Joey will help me clean up, won't you, honey?"

"Can I play in the sink?"

"You can *carry* things to the sink, okay?" She handed him a plate.

"Thanks," Coop said. "Come on, Hope."

She followed him, and they settled onto the couch in front of the fire.

"I'll apologize to Alyssa," Hope said flatly. "Is that what you want to talk about?"

"I think an apology would be good. I'm glad you suggested it. But that's not what I want to discuss. I should have talked to you before I asked Alyssa and the boys to stay with us. I honestly thought you'd love the idea."

Hope frowned. "It's fine, Dad. Really. I'm sorry I made such a big deal earlier. But I *do* know how to cook. Some anyway."

"I know that."

"I mean, it's not like I asked her opinion or anything."

He blew out a breath. "You're bored making easy things like mac and cheese and fish sticks. Alyssa wants to help out, so I asked her to help you cook dinner."

She rolled her eyes. "The beef Stroganoff was pretty bad, wasn't it?"

"Not your best."

"Well, now I know why. I didn't turn down the heat and I didn't stir the bottom of the pan."

"Alyssa would probably like hearing you figured that out."

She sighed dramatically.

"You like having them here sometimes, don't you?"

She shrugged. "Joey's fun most of the time. The baby's cute, even if he hates me. And Alyssa could be a lot worse."

Not exactly a glowing endorsement, but… "What's the matter? You don't like sharing our home?"

"I don't mind that. But sometimes I don't feel like sharing *you*."

Hmm. She had a point. They hadn't spent much time together since Alyssa and the boys arrived, had they? "How much homework do you have?"

"I did it at school. Why?"

"Want to go to the high school basketball game?"

"Just you and me?" She grinned.

"Just you and me."

Her grin disappeared too quickly. "Dad, just so you know, I'm not dreaming about a mother anymore."

"Why not? That's been your dream for a long time."

"I'm getting kinda old for it."

"I don't think you're ever get too old for a mother, kiddo."

"You like Alyssa, don't you?"

He caught himself smiling. "She's a remarkable woman."

Hope's heavy sigh stopped him. "Well, for the record? I liked our life the way it was. I can't wait to go back to just us, okay?"

"I hear you." And he did…loud and clear. But her words surprised him. And for reasons he didn't want to examine too closely, they made his chest heavy with disappointment.

Working on the laptop at the kitchen table, Alyssa kept thinking about Hope's flare of anger when they were cooking dinner. She'd hoped Ben's talk with his daughter would help. But neither of them had met her eyes as they'd hurried off to catch a basketball game, and she was anxious to ask Ben what had happened.

Digger scrambled to his feet. Toenails clicking on the hardwood, he trotted to the back door. Finally, she heard Ben's truck in the driveway. When he and Hope walked into the kitchen, she looked up from the laptop. "How was the game?"

"Great," Ben answered. "I had good company, it was exciting and our team won. Can't get better than that." He gave Hope a look. "Do you have something you want to say, Hope?"

The girl focused on the table. "I'm sorry for being rude earlier."

Alyssa smiled. "I'm sorry if I was too bossy."

"Thanks for teaching me the colander thing and how to keep things from burning."

"You're welcome. We can figure out other things you'd like to cook or bake if you want."

"I guess." She looked up at her dad. "I'm going to bed. See you in the morning."

"Sleep well, kiddo. Fun game."

Hope grinned and hurried away.

Ben watched her go, his forehead creased in a frown.

"You're worried about her?"

"A little. She rarely acts out like that. And it's my own fault. I never got around to talking to her like you suggested." He seemed to be avoiding her eyes.

He wasn't telling her everything. "Does she resent our being here?"

"She's feeling a little overlooked, that's all."

"I'm glad you took her to the ball game. Please don't let the boys and me disturb your regular routine any more than necessary, okay?"

He nodded. "Thanks for understanding. And for calming her down earlier. I appreciate it."

"I can relate to her not wanting to share her father. I still don't like sharing mine."

"So it's an ongoing thing?"

"In my case anyway. But my father never found time to drop everything and spend time with me, so you're already ahead of the game with Hope. You always seem to know what to do."

"Me?" He gave her a questioning look. Sighed. "Not even close."

"That's not the way I see it. Did you learn how to parent from your father?"

"Mostly. But too bad for Hope, there's a lot of trial and error."

"You said your mother left when you were eight. What happened?"

"She went back to her family in Vietnam."

She couldn't help frowning. "What an awful thing for her to do."

"My dad was in the military, so we moved a lot, and he was gone much of the time. He said my mother got so miserable and depressed that her health became an issue."

Poor woman. "It must have been terrible for her to have to choose between her health and her husband and child. Is she still there?"

"They both are. When Dad retired, he joined her. I was in college by then."

"You and Hope have only each other. No wonder she worries about you."

He dropped his gaze. "She doesn't completely trust me."

"Of course, she does. I'm the one she's not sure about."

"Hope's trust issues aren't about you. They're about her mother. And I let her down, too."

"I find that hard to believe."

"It's true." He pulled a chair out from the table and sat in it. "It happened not long after we moved here."

"It's difficult to start over."

"Yeah. Hope was only five." He traced the wood grain in the tabletop with his index finger. "She'd lived her whole life in Chicago with familiar things and people and schedules. I was struggling to save the newspaper. We didn't know anybody. But there are no excuses."

She tried to brace herself for whatever he needed to tell her. "Go on."

He blew out a breath. "It's hard to admit." He searched her face as if seeking her understanding. "In Chicago, I always did background checks on people I hired for child care. But here, I hired Denise without doing one. She was capable, smart. Loved Hope. She'd dress her up and paint her fingernails and toenails and all those feminine things. Hope soon adored her. Everything was great for a while."

He shook his head. "I started trusting her enough to let her keep Hope overnight at her place when I worked into the morning to keep the newspaper afloat or worked on the house. I was overextended or a fool, probably both. I'll never know why I didn't see it coming."

"What do you mean?"

He gave her a tortured look. "Denise was a secret alcoholic."

Chills shook her. "How did you find out?"

"She slipped up a few times—missed things she said she'd cover, like Hope's doctor appointment when she had an ear infection. Or one time, she bought treats for Hope to give her classmates for her birthday, but forgot to deliver them. Then she forgot to drop Hope off at school one morning when Hope spent the night."

He stood, paced across the kitchen and back. "The school called me. Hope answered the door in her pajamas. Denise was passed out on the couch, a half bottle of Scotch open on the floor beside her. I shook her awake and left. Later, she called in a panic when she couldn't find Hope. She didn't even remember I'd been there." He shook his head. "Think of what could have happened to Hope because her dad was too stupid to watch out for her."

"You didn't know, Ben. What happened to Denise?"

He shook his head. "I hear she went back to Dun Harbor and has become a public alcoholic like the rest of her family. Sad. But she had no right to involve my daughter in her addiction."

"No, she didn't."

He sat down again. "Hope wanted a mother so badly, she was destroyed. Add that to her mother's abandonment, and you can understand why she's worried I'll let her down again."

"You trusted somebody you shouldn't have, as it turned out. But you've made solid choices for Hope. I admire you for that."

Ben squinted as if he couldn't believe her.

"Denise must have been more than an alcoholic or you and Hope wouldn't have responded to her."

"Of course she was. I offered to help her get into rehab, but she turned me down. She had no interest in changing."

"Like Shelby?"

He nodded. "I'd had an up close view of addiction. Why didn't I see it with Denise?"

"She was probably very good at hiding it. You are human, you know. What amazes me is you had enough trust to invite us into your home after all you and Hope have gone through."

"I'm glad you're here."

"Me, too."

"You're a great listener. I hope I didn't unload too much on you just now. Not every man would have so little sense to tell a woman he admires about his failures."

He admired her? She wanted to ask him why. Instead, she reached out and clasped his hand in hers, needing to make him feel better. "I know it wasn't easy to tell me about that. But you did the right thing. If you can look at it as a learning experience instead of a failure… I mean…it *is* one of the things that's made you the special man you are now."

Ben looked at her as if considering her words. Then holding her gaze, he brought her hand to his lips and kissed it.

It was the most romantic thing a man had ever done for her.

Chapter Nine

Alyssa lay staring at the ceiling. How could she sleep with so much confusion rattling around inside her about Ben? They'd shared a lot over the past few days. They were becoming close friends. But he'd kissed her hand. It was…surprising. In a good way, but unexpected just the same. He'd looked a little surprised himself.

But then he'd smiled, thanked her for listening and told her he thought she was special, too. Of course, he was referring to her earlier comment about him. And he'd seemed genuinely touched by her encouragement. That was all it was. No need to make any more out of it than that.

But he'd *kissed her hand*. No man had ever done that before. Who knew he was such a romantic? She sighed with the sheer pleasure of it.

Hadn't she had issues with her erratic pulse almost from the beginning? And there was that mysterious connection she'd felt right away. And his smile that always claimed her attention. Hadn't she enjoyed his closeness? Even caught herself flirting with him?

Hmm. She blew out a breath, her confusion dissipating and allowing serious concerns to crowd her mind. Extremely important concerns like her boys and Hope and Ben himself.

And if she needed further discouragement to her thoughts of romance, what about her need to learn to stand on her own and pull her life and her cottage together before her parents came for Christmas? How would romance keep her on track with that?

It wouldn't. Romance was nowhere in the picture. Giving in to a hearty sigh, she turned on her side and repositioned her pillow. She was ready for some serious sleeping now that she had her priorities clearly in place again. No matter how romantic Ben's gesture had been.

Returning from town with a few needed groceries, Alyssa stopped at the cottage mailbox to see if any mail had been forwarded and was surprised there were several pieces, including the monthly envelope from her parents.

The school bus passed her and dropped Hope off. Alyssa got back in her car and drove into Ben's drive.

As soon as Joey was out of the car, he ran to Hope. "Let's play in the snow."

Alyssa watched the exchange a little uneasily. She didn't know where she stood with the girl, and she wanted to be sure Hope didn't take out her anger on Joey.

"Okay," Hope answered. "But we need our snow clothes first." Clasping Joey's hand, they jogged for the house.

She was relieved Joey still seemed to be in Hope's favor. Carrying Robbie in his car seat, Alyssa followed them. She walked into the laundry room and almost ran into the kids scrambling to get into boots and snow clothes with Digger doing his best to help by wagging his entire body for attention smack in everybody's way. "Need anything?"

"We're good." Hope helped Joey switch his boot to the correct foot.

Hope took good care of Joey. No wonder he trusted the girl. By the time Alyssa had unbundled Robbie in the kitchen and taken off her own coat, the kids had grabbed the carrots and charcoal Joey had stashed and were outside putting features on their unfinished snow family.

Alyssa settled on the couch to nurse Robbie. When he fell asleep in her arms, she laid him down, then curled up near him with a cup of tea to browse the decorating magazine she'd bought. It was time to get serious about figuring out what she was going to do about dressing up the cottage. Spying a lovely slipcover, she studied it to determine whether it was simple enough for her to replicate. Maybe. Never mind that she still needed to find a couch to put it on.

She still hoped to have a few furniture pieces in place before her parents came for Christmas. She set her teacup on a side table and shuffled through her mail. Laying aside a couple bills, she opened the envelope from her parents, a check fluttering out. She shook the envelope, always hoping for a letter.

Not surprisingly, it contained only a generous check signed by her father's accountant. The monthly stipend her parents insisted on sending ever since Cam's death, in spite of her objections. She tore it up into small pieces like she always did. Hadn't anybody noticed she never cashed any of them?

Frowning, she jumped up and hurried to get her new cell from her purse. She hit speed dial, settled beside Robbie again and waited.

"This is the Bradley residence."

"Mother, it's Alyssa."

"How wonderful to hear your voice, dear."

"Yours, too."

"I've been trying to call you. I was getting a little worried."

"I'm sorry, Mother. I had to buy a new cell phone."

"How are the boys?"

"They're doing great. Happy and growing fast. We're all fine. You and Daddy?"

"Busy as always."

A warning blinked in the back of her mind. "You're still coming to Wisconsin for Christmas, right?"

"Actually, we don't want to hold you to that invitation given all that's happened over the past year."

"But I want to do it, Mother, especially after everything that's happened." It might not be logical, but a family dinner around Gram's old table was the dream she'd woven and clung to through the darkest times.

"Your father wants to talk to you."

"No. Mom?" Too late. Her mother was already transferring the phone to his home office.

"Alyssa?"

"Hi, Daddy." Deferring to his always-busy schedule, she skipped pleasantries. "I want you and Mother to celebrate Christmas with us at Gram's cottage this year."

"The cottage? It isn't even winterized. And it looked pretty forlorn when your mother and I were there for your grandmother's funeral this past spring."

She hated that she'd had to miss Gram's funeral because she was on bed rest before Robbie was born. Even worse was all the time she'd missed with Gram before she died. "I'm having some work done, so it should be quite comfortable. And I'm really looking forward to serving Christmas dinner on Gram's old kitchen table."

"Your mother didn't tell you? I have to stay in town over Christmas this year. Big meeting I didn't schedule, but I can't miss it either."

She dragged a breath against the familiar hurt. Shouldn't she be used to her parents canceling their plans whenever she tried to do something for them? "But you haven't seen

Robbie since he was two days old. He's going on four months and smiling now. And Joey's growing so fast—"

"Of course, we're anxious to see you and the boys."

"Of course," she said automatically. "Family is important, Daddy."

"I couldn't agree more. Christmas is too far away anyway. That's why we're coming for Thanksgiving."

Thanksgiving? Thanksgiving was in two weeks. Would the cottage even be ready by then?

It would be close. But no way was she going to miss the opportunity for her boys to see their grandparents. Who knew how long it might be before her parents' schedule allowed time again? "Thanksgiving, then. But we won't be in Madison, Daddy. Actually, we're not in Madison now. We're at Rainbow Lake."

"What? But it's almost winter."

"We have lots of snow here already. It's breathtaking."

Silence.

She swallowed around a lump in her throat. She hoped he wasn't reconsidering making the trip. But didn't he always expect her to make her case? "The cottage holds memories of happy times, Daddy. I want to share it with my family. I miss Cam. And Gram," she blurted.

"Well, I guess we'll see you for Thanksgiving at the cottage, then," he said resignedly.

"Thank you, Daddy."

"I only hope we don't have to fly through a blizzard to get there. But we're really looking forward to seeing you and the boys, Lissa. Your mother's been insisting we make the trip for weeks. I just haven't been able to clear my calendar. Now, I'm sorry, but I need to take another call."

"Of course," she said, but he'd already hung up.

Well, they weren't coming for Christmas. And she

wouldn't be as established when they arrived as she'd planned.

But they'd be here for Thanksgiving. The cottage should be mostly done by then. She had a job. And her boys were thriving.

That was just going to have to be established enough for her parents to accept the choices she'd made.

Saturday noon, Coop sat in one of the large circular booths at Della's Main Street Diner with the Reclamation Committee, watching Alyssa jot notes while finishing her salad and running the meeting. Robbie slept contentedly in his carrier beside her. She was a talented woman clearly in her element and loving it.

He smiled to himself, remembering the surprise in her eyes when he'd kissed her hand that night in the kitchen. He had to admit he'd shocked himself, too. But she'd moved him deeply with her compassion and support when he'd admitted he'd contributed to Hope's inability to trust by failing to check Denise's background.

Now, Alyssa pushed away her salad plate and checked her notes. "Looks like that about does it for now."

With murmurs of satisfaction on the progress they'd made toward the fund-raiser and thanks to Alyssa for organizing it, everybody filed out. Everybody except Lou who was folding up the beautiful quilt she'd finished for the silent auction.

"Thank you for bringing your quilt to show us, Lou." Alyssa packed up her things. "I for one will be bidding on it for my bedroom."

Coop made a mental note to keep an eye on the quilt at the silent auction.

"And what little girl wouldn't want some of those doll clothes you made?" Alyssa said.

"They come together pretty quickly, so I'll make more."

Lou finished wrapping her quilt in the cloth she'd brought it in. "You sure do have a contented baby."

Alyssa smiled. "He's such a sweetheart. Thankfully, Hope is practicing her babysitting skills on Joey for a little while. He wouldn't have been nearly as contented for the meeting."

"Once kids start getting around, watch out," Lou said. "Great job planning for the fund-raiser, Alyssa."

"Thanks for agreeing to head the silent auction."

"No problem. Gotta go. We don't want Harold to start beeping the horn out there." Lou hurried away.

Alyssa put the black, wooden toy horse that Max had patterned after Harold's horse, Jack, into her bag. Turning to Coop, she said, "Joey will love this. It was so generous of Max to give it to him."

Della stopped at the booth and began clearing the table. "The announcement in the *Courier* and the posters around town are creating a buzz for the fund-raiser. Ticket sales have been brisk. How's the planning going?"

"Very well," Alyssa answered.

"You can put me down for pies for the bake sale," Della volunteered.

Alyssa smiled. "Thanks, Della."

"My pleasure."

Coop realized time alone with Alyssa was a rare occurrence he wasn't ready to lose. "You want a piece of pie, Alyssa? I'm buying."

She checked her watch. "I think we should check with Hope first, in case she's tired of watching Joey."

"I doubt she is, but I'll call to make sure." While Alyssa and Della visited, he hit speed dial, checked in with Hope and signed off. "She says everything's great. She's reading, and Joey's taking his nap."

"Wow. In that case, do you have gooseberry pie this time of year?" Alyssa asked.

"Sure do," Della answered. "Several regulars wouldn't have any other kind, and we always have plenty of gooseberries around here and plenty of pickers looking to sell them for me to freeze. I'll get you both some pie if you like."

"Make mine pecan," Coop said. "With ice cream. Alyssa?"

She nodded.

Della hustled off to fill their orders.

Coop moved closer to Alyssa in the giant booth. "Never would have thought you'd like gooseberries. Too sour for me."

"I love their tartness. Gram used to take me gooseberry picking and bake pies with our harvest. So good. We picked gooseberries on an older couple's farm. Friends of Gram. Sometimes, we'd get watercress there, too." She laughed.

"What's so funny?"

"One day, Gram reached too far and fell in the creek, and the man pulled her out. The water was so cold, spring fed, she said. Anyway, the water temperature made my hands hurt, so I was worried about her. But Gram and her friends thought the whole thing was hilarious."

Coop chuckled, enjoying hearing Alyssa's happy memories with Emma.

"Oh." Alyssa frowned. "I forgot to ask Lou about thrift shops in town. Do you know anything about them?"

"Locals say the best selection and deals can be had at Fred's Antiques and Collectibles. I hear Fred lives to bargain with his customers."

"Does he ever." Della approached the booth, a plate of pie à la mode in each hand. She set the plates on the table in front of them. "People tease Fred about being independently wealthy and in business only to bargain." She bustled away.

Alyssa took a bite of her dessert. "Mmm."

Coop nodded, swallowing his mouthful of ice cream. "You planning to shop for furniture at a thrift store?"

"If I can find a decent sofa, I'm going to try to sew a slip-cover for it. I'm thinking I'll stick with cottage chic." She took another bite of pie.

He ate his pie, but he couldn't deny his attention was focused on the woman sitting in the booth with him. Sure, he saw her at home, but seldom without the kids around. He loved the kids, but he was enjoying having her to himself for a change. "I have no idea what 'cottage chic' is. Sounds intriguing, though."

"All I know about it, I saw in a decorating magazine. It looks child-friendly, and I think it will suit my budget. Anyway, it reminds me of the way Gram kept the cottage, so I love that." She took another bite.

"Let me know when you want to go shopping, and I'll drive you. That way, you'll have my truck to haul home what you buy."

Alyssa blinked. "I didn't think of that. But I've never been in a thrift shop before, so I don't know that I'll be able to find anything I need. You certainly have more important things to do than browse in a thrift shop with me."

"No."

"No?"

"Can't think of a thing."

"But it will probably have to be during your work hours."

"I don't chain myself to the newspaper, you know. So unless you'd rather shop alone, might be fun."

"Then you're on." She went back to finishing off her dessert, then suddenly looked up. "You know what?"

He shook his head.

"I'm pretty sure Gram's friends, that older couple I mentioned?"

He nodded.

"I think they were Zebadiah and his wife, Viola. I'll have to ask him."

"Want to stop there on the way home?"

"Do you think Hope will mind if we stop for a few minutes?"

"She'll be fine. Shouldn't take long. You think Zebadiah will answer the door if I'm with you?"

"I have no idea."

"Well, can't hurt to give it a try."

"Okay. I think I'll take a gooseberry pie to him."

A short time later, gripping Robbie's carrier, Coop stood beside Alyssa on Zebadiah's wraparound porch.

Pie in hand, she knocked on the door. "Zebadiah, it's Alyssa, Emma and Charlie's granddaughter. I brought Ben Cooper with me. Remember, I told you I'd like you to meet him?"

Silence.

Alyssa turned to Coop.

He raised his eyebrows. "I don't hear anything, do you?"

Shaking her head, she turned back to the door. "I have one of Della's gooseberry pies for you. It's delicious. Made me think of you and Viola and Gram. She used to bring me to your farm to pick gooseberries, didn't she?"

Still no sound inside.

"Do you remember the day Gram fell in the creek trying to get watercress? And Viola was there. And you pulled Gram out. That was you, wasn't it?"

The door slowly opened, and Zebadiah stood there with his grumpy face on as usual. "I didn't think anybody but me remembered my Viola."

"She was as pretty as her name. That was me with Gram. When I was a little girl," she said excitedly.

"You sure were a serious little thing. So worried Emma would catch a cold."

"I was. I loved her so much."

Coop was touched by the interaction between Alyssa

and the reclusive old man. Judging by the way Zebadiah responded to her, Coop wasn't the only one who sensed her depth and compassion.

Zebadiah looked at Coop as if he'd just noticed him. "You the Cooper who runs the *Courier?*"

"That's right." Coop offered his hand. "I'm Ben Cooper. Glad to meet you."

Zebadiah frowned at Coop's hand, then reached out with a strong grip. "You come to take a look at my generator?"

"Sure."

"Don't want this little lady to worry about me. She's just like Emma."

Coop grinned. "She cares about you. Want to show me that generator?"

A half hour later, Coop drove toward home, Zebadiah's ancient generator in the back of his truck. Because its problems were beyond Coop's expertise, he'd convinced Zebadiah to let him take it to a repair shop with the promise that he'd have it or a new one back before the next storm.

But right now, he was fortunate his truck knew the way home because the woman beside him held his full attention. He was really enjoying her excited chatter about Zebadiah's "breakthrough," as she called the old man's asking Coop for help with the generator. He searched his mind to figure out a way to spend time with her again without the kids. "You ever snowshoe?"

She shook her head.

"Want to try it?"

"Sure. Sounds like fun."

"Lots of fun. I was thinking, snowshoeing is probably the best way to get those Christmas trees for the fund-raiser from Harold and Lou's tree farm."

"Great. Does Hope snowshoe?"

"Too slow for her. She likes to ski."

"Can we take the boys with us?"

He met her eyes. "Wouldn't work the greatest, especially pulling the trees out after we cut them."

"Oh. Right." She nodded in understanding, but she held his gaze a little too long.

Was she trying to figure him out? Or was she realizing that snowshoeing would mean they'd be alone? "Will it be too soon to get the trees tomorrow afternoon while the committee is working on the Victorian? We can leave the kids with them for a while."

"The fund-raiser is only two weeks away, so getting trees tomorrow should be fine."

Thankfully, she didn't object to being alone with him. That fact gave him a little jolt of confidence. Maybe he wasn't out on this limb all by himself after all. He'd like to believe that.

Because the more he got to know her, the more time he wanted to spend with her. In spite of Hope's closed attitude. Would she change her mind? What if she didn't? He blew out a breath.

"Something wrong?" Alyssa asked. "You sound worried."

"Sorry."

"Can I help? Somebody told me recently I'm a good listener. Oh, yeah, it was you," she teased.

"Just a problem at work," he fibbed. Better to fib than to hurt her feelings by telling her his daughter couldn't wait for her to move out. Hurting either her or Hope wasn't something he ever wanted to do.

Chapter Ten

A fire crackled in the fireplace. Smells of pumpkin cookies Alyssa baked after she and Ben returned from the committee meeting and seeing Zebadiah filled the house. Hope had opted out of baking but had helped with cooking supper. Ben hadn't given his daughter a choice about stringing popcorn for the fund-raiser's Christmas trees.

With so much to do before Thanksgiving weekend, Alyssa could certainly use the help. She carefully pushed a popcorn kernel along her length of thread.

"This is really a dumb idea," Hope grumped from the other end of the couch. "My popcorn broke again."

"Give it a little patience," Ben coached from his chair by the fire. "Now that I have the hang of it, I'm making up for lost time."

"I don't think my garland will be a foot long." Hope grabbed a handful of popcorn from the big stainless-steel bowl on the hassock and bent her head over her needle and thread again.

"Oops. Looks pretty crooked." Ben held up his twisted, squiggly garland and peered seriously at it.

Alyssa tried to squelch her smile. He was trying so hard. "Do you think you could be pulling the thread too tight?"

"Maybe that's it." He set about trying to loosen it. "How many of these things are we making?"

"Thirty or so should be enough."

His head shot up. "Are you kidding?"

"Afraid not. I've never made one before either, which is why I'm very glad for your help."

"And we're happy to lend a hand." He flashed his irresistible grin.

Which didn't help at all. Because all she could do was grin right back.

He chuckled.

Even worse. Because, of course, all she could do was chuckle.

"What's so funny?" Hope asked.

"It's sad, really." Ben ditched his smile. "This garland is proof positive that I don't have a crafty cell in my body."

"I don't either," Hope said glumly.

"Neither do I." Alyssa held up her perfectly centered eight popcorn kernels. "At this rate, maybe I can make a six-foot string by Christmas. Maybe."

"Let's hire somebody to do it for us," Hope suggested.

"Even if we could find somebody to hire, we'd never live it down," Ben said.

"What's really sad is Lou wouldn't even consider this a craft. That's probably why she thinks we can do it."

They all laughed, which was better than grumping any day.

"Thirty or so." Ben made a face. "We'd better hunker down and figure out what we're doing."

"I just remembered, I have a book report due."

"When?"

"Next week," Hope mumbled. "Unfortunately."

Ben shot his daughter a sardonic look. "Nice try."

Joey zoomed through the living room, arms raised to

fly Braveman to the rescue, then he zoomed back into the kitchen. Digger's toenails clicked on the hardwood as he trotted to keep up with the boy.

Robbie cooed and kicked in his Pack 'N Play, making sure he was part of the excitement.

"Alyssa, I've been meaning to ask where your parents are staying when they come for Thanksgiving," Ben said.

"In the cottage with us. I called the B and B, but Mrs. Hendrickson is still recuperating."

"They're welcome to use my guest room."

"I appreciate your offer, but I'll give them my room, and I'll sleep on the sofa I hope to buy before then."

"Maybe you can find a hide-a-bed," Ben suggested.

"That's a good idea. I'll have to see."

"Well, the guest room-offer stands, so if you change your mind, let me know."

"I'm doing the nursery at church tomorrow," Hope said. "Can I ask Joey if he wants to come with me?"

Alyssa looked up from her project. "I think he'd love it, Hope." She thought about church. She'd dealt with some of her emotions regarding Cam's funeral with her visits to the sanctuary this week. Could she handle going to a service? She hoped so. "I think Robbie and I will tag along to church with you, too, if that's okay."

Ben looked up, smiled. "Great. We'd love to have you."

"When are you moving to your cottage?" Hope asked brightly.

"Tony says he's right on schedule, so it should be done in another week."

"We're going to miss you and the boys," Ben said kindly.

"We'll miss you and Hope, too."

Hope kept her head down, working harder than ever on her garland.

Well, she couldn't blame Hope for wanting her dad to herself again. She was glad Ben hadn't prodded his daughter to say something she didn't feel. That would be even harder to deal with than Hope's obvious silence.

"Good morning." Glad to have made it through the service with a minimum of tears, Alyssa reached out to shake Pastor Nick's hand.

"Good morning, Alyssa." He smiled at Robbie who'd slept through the entire service. "Looks like I put your baby to sleep."

Alyssa smiled. "You gave *me* a lot to think about."

"Yes?"

She nodded and moved on.

"Great message." Ben shook the pastor's hand.

Ben walked with Alyssa toward the nursery to collect Joey and Hope. "Did you enjoy the sermon?"

Was he asking a rhetorical question? Not normally his style. Still…

He chuckled. "Your silence is deafening."

"I'm not sure how to answer your question," she explained honestly.

"The truth would work."

"Well, how can we ever live up to God's expectations?"

"What do you mean?"

"'Inasmuch as ye have done it unto the least of these… ye have done it unto me.'" She drew a breath. "Essentially, Jesus is saying we are our brother's keeper."

"Essentially. God *is* perfect love."

She nodded. "But that's what He expects from us? Perfect love?"

"That's what He wants *for* us because He loves us. He wants us to rely on Him because with Him, all things are possible."

She nodded. "I'm afraid I have a long way to go."

"Don't we all?" He opened the nursery room door for her to step inside.

Joey ran up to them. "Hope says we can have doughnuts in the fellship room."

Alyssa looked to Ben for verification.

"He's right. Hope needs to stay until all the parents pick up their children. Then she has Sunday school. But I'll take you and the boys home whenever you want to leave." He motioned to his daughter. "Pick you up later."

She nodded as she helped a cute little girl with red pigtails into her jacket.

Alyssa smiled at Hope, but the girl turned away. She should be used to Hope's big freeze by now, but it hurt every time. Would she ever find a way to reach her? Maybe when she moved?

"Do you know where the doughnuts are, Ben?" Joey asked excitedly.

"Sure do." Guiding Alyssa and Joey down the hall, Ben turned to her, concern in his eyes. "Doing okay?"

She smiled. "Doing fine."

"I'm sure it wasn't easy."

Had he seen her tears? She reached out and laid her hand on his arm to let him know she appreciated his concern. "It's mostly the hymns that get me."

He nodded as if he understood. "Music can do that."

They walked into the fellowship room abuzz with people. A bank of windows allowed a lot of natural light into the generous room. Several murals of biblical scenes graced the walls, and a stone fireplace stood in one corner with a cluster of comfortable chairs facing it. Another corner sported children's tables and chairs. Several adult-size tables laden with goodies were pulled away from the wall and spaced for easy access. Alyssa began helping Joey make his choice.

Ben laid his hand on her shoulder to get her attention. "I need to talk to some people about the Burkhalter project."

With his touch stealing her breath, she met his gaze.

His rich brown eyes crinkled in a smile just for her, and warmth flushed her neck and cheeks.

Not good. She glanced nervously away. Why was she reacting this way?

Questioning her with his eyes, he took his hand from her shoulder. "You okay?"

She seriously doubted it, but she nodded anyway.

"I won't be long." Frowning, he turned and walked away.

Drawing a stabilizing breath, she lifted her fingers to her burning cheeks and glanced around to get her bearings.

"Mommy, I want that one and that one and that one." Joey pointed out his choices.

Alyssa scrambled to switch into mother mode. "Uh, Joey, let's start with one doughnut."

"But I'm really hungry," Joey whined.

"If you're still hungry after you eat one, you can choose another one."

"'Kay. Then I want that one." He pointed to a chocolate doughnut with gooey frosting and colorful sprinkles, the biggest, messiest concoction on the entire serving tray.

"I think you found the very best one, Joey." EMT Liz looked at Alyssa. "Is everything okay?"

"Yes, of course."

"You look a little…flustered." Liz gave her a puzzled look. "Here, while you juggle the baby, let me set Joey up at one of the kids' tables."

Alyssa shook her head to object, but Liz already had Joey and his sticky doughnut well in hand. Appearing to need help was the last thing she wanted. She grabbed plenty of extra napkins and followed Liz to the corner of children's tables. "Thanks."

"You're welcome. Good to see you. Sorry, but I have to rush off to teach Sunday school now." Liz hurried away.

"You have such a darling baby." The young woman who'd offered to help Alyssa at Ben's newspaper office held a cup of coffee out to her. "Would you like this?"

She shook her head. "It's too difficult to drink it with the baby."

"That's okay. I'll drink it myself." She took a sip. "I'm Sharon Applegate. I work for Ben Cooper."

"I remember you."

"Have you known him a long time?"

"Not long." Alyssa frowned. She certainly hadn't known him long enough to account for her unexplainable reaction to his touch a few minutes ago.

"Did you know him in Chicago before he moved here?"

"No, I didn't."

The young woman gave her a questioning look. "But you must be old friends. You and your children are staying with him, right?"

Were Ben's employees curious about his private life? At least, Sharon Applegate seemed to be. But if she thought she'd learn anything from Alyssa, she was mistaken. "You have a beautiful church," she commented.

Sharon's eyes widened as she realized Alyssa's change of topic. "Yes. I think so, too."

"Hi, Sharon." Ben stopped at Alyssa's side.

Did she sense a new intimacy between Ben and herself or was it only her imagination? To be safe, Alyssa forbade herself from responding to him in any way. The last thing either of them needed was people gossiping.

Sharon offered him a bright smile.

But Ben's attention was on Joey. "Looks like he needs help." He leaned to wipe Joey's face and hands with the napkins Alyssa had provided, then he lifted Joey from his little chair and hurried off with him. "Bathroom to clean him up," he called over his shoulder.

The practical matter of a small boy's encounter with chocolate overriding her anxiety, Alyssa wanted to cheer for Ben's quick thinking. "Sticky doughnuts and little boys are a disaster in the making."

Sharon turned appraising eyes on Alyssa. "Well, it's nice seeing you again." She walked away.

Alyssa closed her eyes. Was Sharon interested in Ben as more than an employer? Or he in her, for that matter? But hadn't he said he hadn't dated for a long time? Why was she wondering about his relationship with the single women in town? He was a young, vibrant man. Of course, he must be interested even if he didn't date. And why wouldn't they be interested in him, tall, dark, handsome, single father that he was?

But there was a lot more to Ben than his appearance. He was a complex, warm, exciting man with a heart too big for his own good and a daughter who needed all his attention and did not welcome outsiders.

And Alyssa? She was still a new widow with two little boys to provide for and raise while doing her very best to grow into the strong woman she longed to become. Nowhere in that mix did she see room for a relationship.

And she was really beginning to regret that.

The air was crisp. Flashes of sun glinted through tree branches heavy with snow. The shoosh of their snowshoes, the swish of the toboggan tied to Coop's waist and the scuttle of an occasional small animal were the only sounds in the woods.

Coop was sweating bullets in spite of the cold temperature. Breaking trail through new snow burned a ton of energy. Which was probably helpful considering how much he'd been looking forward to whisking Alyssa away from the decorating extravaganza going on at the Victorian.

He didn't begin to understand what had happened between them in the fellowship room this morning. One minute everything was normal, the next…he'd been lost in Alyssa looking at him as if seeing him for the first time and really liking what she saw.

Or was that only what he longed to believe? He glanced back at her, a smile winding through him. Looked like she was handling her snowshoes well. They were a little big for her weight, which should help her in the new snow that had fallen overnight. Stopping to rest a minute, he dropped his poles and wriggled his backpack off his shoulders. He ripped off his jacket and stuffed it in the backpack. "How's it going?"

She stopped a few feet away. "Good. My calf muscles are complaining, though."

"Mine, too. They always do the first couple times each winter. It looks like you're following my instructions."

"I'm trying." She took a few steps to demonstrate.

"Looking good." Was he kidding? She looked amazing in her short, blue parka that matched her eyes and a jaunty, blue-and-green plaid hat and scarf. Dark blue snow pants hugged her legs, and Eskimo boots looked as if they'd stand up to the weather. A vision to behold. "You could try exaggerating your stride a little more."

She took a few practice strides. Stopped. Looked to him for suggestions.

"Perfect." He wanted to show her anyway, but he had a feeling it would only be an excuse to be closer to her. Turning, he pointed to small hoofprints in the snow. "Deer."

"Do you think they're watching us?"

"Could be. Maybe we're traipsing through their living room." He looked down the steep hill. "That's the grove where Harold told us the Frasers are."

"How do we get down there?"

"I'll break a trail. Then you can sit on your snowshoes and slide down."

"Sounds like cheating."

"It's called glissading. You'll rest your leg muscles and pack the trail at the same time, so it will be easier to bring the trees up the hill later. All you have to do is remember to keep the toes of the shoes up."

She nibbled her bottom lip in that way she did.

He couldn't look away. He strode to her. "Let me take your poles."

Avoiding his eyes, she handed them to him.

Why couldn't she meet his eyes? Was she struggling with their being alone, too? He'd sure like to think so. Not that it helped him keep his mind on the task at hand. He clumsily tied her poles to his backpack with the saw, then lifted the pack onto his shoulders. "See you at the bottom of the hill."

He grabbed his poles and took off running downhill in exaggerated steps, using his poles as he slid slightly on the snow. The toboggan tugging at his waist challenged his balance, but he soon got the hang of it. Reaching the bottom, he motioned for Alyssa to slide down.

She came flying, squealing and laughing all the way.

He laughed with her. It was great watching her have a good time for a change. To be young and free and unencumbered by the disappointments and hardships she'd had to deal with.

She stopped a few feet past him, stood and brushed snow off her snow pants, her face flushed and exuberant. "That was fun!"

Chuckling, he covered the ground between them, ready to give her a hug. Instead, he dumped his backpack on the toboggan and began untying her poles and the saw from it. "You like snowshoeing?"

"I do. Especially glissading." She threw her arms open as if to embrace her surroundings. "How could I not love getting out in the middle of all this?"

"My sentiments exactly." The thought of walking into her outstretched arms nudged his mind. He managed to squelch the idea and hand her the ski poles. He motioned to the stand of pine not far away. "Shall we go cut the perfect tree for the Stefanos' Victorian?"

"Let's do it." She strode beside him.

He pointed at a great-looking spruce. "How about that one?"

"Too fat."

"Too *fat?* I wasn't aware we were looking for a skinny tree."

"Tall and skinny and full. But not so full that it interferes with traffic flow in the foyer. It has to fit in that space by the stairs. I have exact measurements in my pocket."

Of course she did.

"Besides, that tree isn't a Fraser fir."

"Right. I wouldn't recognize a Fraser if I saw it."

"They're a tad bluer and have flatter needles."

"You're an expert on trees, too? Why doesn't that surprise me?"

"I do know my Christmas trees."

He grinned at the saucy confidence in her tone and squelched the urge to hug her…again. A hug could easily lead to a kiss, his mind argued. Not helpful. He pointed at a tree that might fit the bill. "What about that one?"

She gave her head a shake and kept walking, scanning the woods.

Was she as occupied with finding a tree as she appeared? Had kissing even entered her mind? Once or twice anyway?

"Do you think there will be enough room on the toboggan for the tree for the Victorian and the one for the fellowship room? Or will we have to come back?"

Time alone another day? He liked the sound of that. "I vote for coming back, but we can see if we have room once we find one for the Victorian. Will you have time this week for another trip?"

"I have several projects in the works for the cottage and for the fund-raiser. Not sure how many I'll finish before Thanksgiving. And I still need to shop for a couch. But if we need to make another trip…"

He smiled. "I vote for another trip."

She smiled back. "Me, too. It will be fun."

"I was thinking, it's kind of nice being alone," he admitted. "Without the kids."

"Yes, it is." Without warning, she veered off and disappeared into the trees.

"Alyssa?" He didn't know where she'd disappeared to, but she had agreed it was nice being alone with him. He wanted to whoop for joy. He quickly untied the toboggan from his belt and went after her, saw in hand.

She stood studying the attributes of a tall, slim fir.

He moved to stand beside her, then looked at the tree she'd been studying. "Is this it?"

"No." She moved on.

He followed her, doing his best to keep the mood light when he wanted so much more. "That tree didn't meet your tall, skinny, full criteria? Or wasn't it a Fraser fir?"

"It was a good Fraser for the fellowship room. But we need one with more presence for the Victorian. Probably a foot taller. The Victorian has ten-foot ceilings, you know."

He knew the ceilings were high, but he hadn't measured the way she had.

She walked deeper into the woods, stopping to assess a tree now and then and moving on.

He followed, the trees too thick for him to walk beside her.

A startled rabbit took off, leaving a trail in the pristine snow.

"This one is nice." She used her poles to maneuver around the tree to get a better look. "What do you think?"

He shrugged. "Looks perfect." But then, so had several others, so what did he know?

Laying down her poles, she crouched to look under the tree. "That trunk looks like it will take a while to saw through."

"So this is the one?"

"This is it." She flashed a smile.

The smile catching him totally off guard, he shot her a helpless grin he didn't have the presence of mind to hide.

Her gaze seemed to snag and hold. Her smiling eyes growing serious, she made a little sound that zinged straight to his heart.

Did that small sound mean he wasn't the only one struggling with feelings? Or that she recognized that he was battling with his? He didn't waste another guess as to what she might be thinking. Stumbling in his snowshoes, he managed to move closer.

She squinted in a worried kind of way.

But worried wasn't what he was looking for. Not even close. She clearly wasn't ready for his kiss, no matter how much he wanted her to be. Raising the saw in a victorious gesture he didn't feel, he turned away and blustered ahead. "Ready to cut the perfect tree?"

"I'm sorry," she answered quietly.

Dragging a breath, he turned back to her. "It's okay," he lied. Doing his best to accept his disappointment, he went to work.

Chapter Eleven

The boys long asleep, Digger jumped up and raced for the back door before Alyssa heard Ben's truck in the driveway. She'd been thinking about him all evening. Reliving the moment yesterday in the woods when she'd realized he meant to kiss her. She'd panicked.

She drew a deep breath. The problem was, she'd wanted his kiss.

But she couldn't want that. Hope would be so upset. But Hope wasn't the only reason. Alyssa couldn't let her feelings for Ben get in the way of learning to live on her own terms. Not this time. Not even with Ben Cooper, no matter how much she admired him or wanted to kiss him.

She deposited the final bag of cookies she'd baked for the fund-raiser into the freezer drawer. Her plan to bake with Hope after they'd cooked dinner together had fallen by the wayside when she learned Hope had a school ski trip with Ben acting as one of the chaperones. A good experience for them. She was glad he was keeping up with his daughter's scheduled activities.

But Alyssa wanted to do something to put Hope more at ease with her, which didn't seem to be happening while she taught the girl the finer points of cooking. If only she could figure out what might help. Leaning against the counter, she picked up her cup of tea and thoughtfully took a sip.

Ben and Hope slammed into the mudroom, continuing their conversation while they climbed out of their snow gear.

"Why can't I, Dad? Stephanie's mom said it was okay."

"I'm not Stephanie's mom," Ben calmly answered.

"Oh! That is so irritating when you do that." Hope's voice took on a defiant tone. "Give me one good reason."

"I told you, I don't want you mutilating yourself."

Mutilating herself? What did Hope want? A tattoo?

"You're the only person in the whole world who thinks that," Hope huffed. "Doesn't that bother you at all?"

"No, even if it were true."

"Well, it bothers *me* a lot. Sometimes it's like you live in the dark ages."

Alyssa cringed, wanting to rush in and defend Ben. Wouldn't *that* go over well with Hope? She doubted he would appreciate it either.

"Do you have homework that needs doing before bed?" Ben asked quietly.

"I did it at school," Hope grumped.

"Good job." He strode into the kitchen, his cheeks ruddy from the outdoors, his strong, lean body seemingly coiled for action. Shaking his head, he met Alyssa's gaze.

She gave him an encouraging look.

Hope marched across the kitchen and took the milk out of the refrigerator.

Alyssa pointed to the table. "I put a plate of cookies out if you two are hungry."

Hope silently continued fixing a mug of hot chocolate.

"Thanks, Alyssa." Ben grabbed a couple cookies off the plate on the table. "Sure smells good in here, doesn't it, Hope?"

"I'm not hungry." Waiting for her hot chocolate to heat in the microwave, she stared at Alyssa.

"Did you have fun skiing?"

Hope shrugged. "Most of my friends weren't there."

"They don't like to ski?"

"They're too scared to try."

"We could take a few of your friends to a hill with us." Ben reached for another cookie. "I could give them some pointers. Maybe then, they'd feel more comfortable going with the group."

"I can ask." Hope shrugged, but she sounded a little more positive. After the microwave bell pinged, she retrieved her mug. "Dad, have you noticed Alyssa's ears?"

Alyssa put her hand to her ear. "What about my ears?"

Hope focused intently on her. "How old were you when you had your ears pierced?"

Uh-oh. Hope wanted to get her ears pierced? Alyssa had the sinking feeling she wasn't going to win points from Hope with her answer. On the bright side, she wouldn't thwart Ben's plan for his daughter either. "I had my ears pierced when I graduated from law school. It was a present to myself, you might say."

Hope glowered at her.

"My father felt as strongly about it as yours seems to, Hope," she said honestly.

"It figures." Hope gulped down her hot chocolate.

"If it's any consolation, it hurts more than you think it will. And you have to clean your ears with alcohol several times a day. If you don't, you can get an infection and have to let your ears heal shut, then get them pierced again when they're healthy."

"Is that really true?" Hope gave her a squeamish look.

"A friend of mine had that problem."

"But yours were fine, right?"

"I was supercareful because of my friend's story, believe me."

"Stephanie's careful, and so am I. That's not gonna happen to us." Hope rinsed her mug and put it in the dishwasher.

"That's right, because you're not getting your ears pierced, kiddo."

Head down, Hope hurried out of the room.

Ben took another cookie. "These are really good."

"I'm glad you like them."

He walked to the refrigerator. "I'm sorry you got caught in the middle of that."

"It's hard being twelve."

"If only she wasn't in such a hurry to grow up." He poured a glass of milk.

"You should be glad I didn't get my ears pierced when I was twelve."

"There is that. What is it about kids getting their ears pierced anyway? Is it because other kids are doing it? Is it a rite of passage, something that makes them feel more independent and grown-up?"

"There are probably lots of reasons. By the time I did it, it was a practical solution. Those clip-on earrings really hurt."

He studied her. "Yours look nice, by the way."

"Thank you." She felt her neck and cheeks heat up. *Oh, please.* She needed to get over herself.

He took a drink of milk. "Thanks for being concerned about her in spite of the way she's been treating you."

"Of course, I'm concerned. She's sharing you with my boys and me 24/7."

"But I'm right here, and I'm not going anywhere. Why can't she see that?"

"I don't know. I doubt she knows what's wrong either. She just feels it and acts out."

"I'm really sorry about her rudeness."

"I can take it. I'm a big girl, you know."

"I know."

Heat flushed her neck and cheeks. Again.

"I also know a big girl's feelings can be hurt just like a little girl's. I'm sorry my daughter's hurting you."

The sincerity in his eyes made her tremble inside. He truly cared how she felt.

Oh, she was in so much trouble. Had he noticed?

The tension in his jaw softened into a smile that kept getting broader.

He'd noticed, all right. Wasn't *that* a comforting thought?

"Elegant? It's straight out of the seventies. Are you sure that's the one Fred told us to look at?" Alyssa pointed through the gloom of Fred's Antiques and Collectibles at an old couch covered in very large gold, green and brown floral fabric.

Ben strode to the couch, lifted one of the cushions and turned to Alyssa. "Yup. This is the brand Fred said lasts forever." He pushed on the firm back and springs as if proving his point. "And it's a hide-a-bed. What it lacks in beauty, it makes up for in function."

"The store owner's interpretation of 'elegant' is more than a little alarming," she grumbled.

Joey sneezed.

The dusty shop made Alyssa want to sneeze, too. Balancing Robbie in one arm, she grasped a tissue from her purse and helped Joey blow his nose.

Ben had whipped out a tape measure and was measuring the ugly couch.

Alyssa glanced at the door, ready to chalk up her one-and-only trip to a thrift store as a waste of time.

"It should fit your space perfectly." Ben looked up from the drawing of the cottage floor plan Alyssa had sketched.

She shook her head in distaste. "But it's so…ugly."

"Don't you plan to sew a slipcover for it?"

"I'm going to try."

"Then it will be beautiful as well as functional."

"Well, passable maybe. You have more confidence in my sewing abilities than I do."

"It's all about seeing beyond first impressions." Fred strolled up to them. "It's fun to see what fabric and paint and imagination combined with elbow grease can do to transform ugly into beautiful. And for not much money."

Alyssa tried to visualize the couch as anything but the beast it was and failed.

"Trust me, this is a real find," Fred assured. "And the price is already good, but I'm always disappointed if I don't get the chance to bargain with my customers."

Remembering Della's comment about Fred, Alyssa shot Ben a look.

He smiled.

Immediately, everything seemed better. How did he do that? "Tony will have the cottage ready to move into in less than a week," she said. "The problem is, I'll have to use the sofa like it is until I have time to sew a slipcover. And I don't see that happening before Thanksgiving."

"Well, it has good Thanksgiving colors," Fred pointed out.

"Hmm. You're right. I didn't think of that," Alyssa admitted. "The cottage will be mostly neutral shades, so I suppose…"

Ben lifted Joey to straddle his shoulders. "Why don't you think about the couch while we look around? Maybe we can find more great stuff."

"Like what?" Alyssa asked uncertainly.

"I don't know yet. Let's use our imaginations."

"Have fun. Let me know if you need me." Fred drifted away to talk to another customer.

"What about this?"

"The lamp?" She looked at the tattered lampshade with a skeptical eye.

Ben whipped off the shade. "See? If you like the lamp, you can buy a new shade."

She squinted at the lamp as if that might help. It did have good lines, didn't it? "You're right. It could be great, but where would I buy a new shade?"

"I've seen a few at the hardware store. Pretty reasonable." He held up the price tag for her to see. "Don't forget, Fred likes to bargain."

She nodded. "Sold."

He laughed. "Want to see what else he has?"

"What about that old trunk over there? If I polish it up, I think it will make a perfect coffee table. It will even add storage in the living room."

"Clever." He shot her a grin.

She grinned right back. "I think I'm beginning to see possibilities."

"I never doubted you." He peered around the store. "What about that large piece of furniture against the wall?"

"The armoire? It's amazing." She walked over to get a closer look.

Ben stroked the beautiful dark wood. "Looks like walnut to me."

"It's so rich-looking. It would be perfect in my bedroom for storage. The closet in there is so tiny." She turned over the price tag. "A little pricey, but I really like it."

"Want to see how much we can bargain the price down?"

She nodded. After adding a couple battered, wooden chairs and a pair of funky car bookends for Joey, she decided the couch was growing on her. So Fred, the friendly proprietor, began bargaining with her until she wanted to just write a check and be done with it.

That was when the determined and thrifty Ben she hadn't seen before took over and hung in there until he got a low price for the lot plus free delivery when the cottage was ready.

As it turned out, they wouldn't need his truck to haul things after all. Alyssa had fun with Ben and even learned a few things about him. And about bargaining. And they all walked away satisfied with the deal.

She still didn't have a clear vision of cottage chic, but it sounded fun and within her budget. A winning solution to her furniture problem.

Thursday afternoon, with the smell and humidity of fresh paint making her nose itch, Alyssa stretched to roll paint on her bedroom wall. She'd accomplished a lot while the boys napped, but there was still way too much to do to be ready to move into the cottage Saturday. The biggest problem? She was feeling shaky about leaving Ben and his wonderful home. How strong was that? Gram would be ashamed.

"Anybody home?" Ben's deep voice came from the hall.

He triggered a sense of anticipation in her before she even saw him. Not good. "You're home early."

"I thought maybe I could help out with something before your big move Saturday." He walked into the small room and glanced around. "Wow!"

"It's mango punch. Do you think it's too bright?"

He shrugged. "Should be a cheerful color to wake up to."

"I'm picking up one of the minor colors in Lou's quilt, just in case I can afford to buy it. I love most shades of pink. But I wanted more punch than feminine."

He looked around. "I like it."

She grinned. "You have no idea what I'm babbling about, do you?"

"Decorating stuff, you mean?"

"Decorating stuff?" she teased.

Grinning, he threw up his hands as if at a loss. "You're making a lot of progress here."

"Now that I'm getting the knack of it. I put stew in the crockpot for dinner."

"Great. I love stew."

He was so easy to please. "I'm trying to finish painting before it's time to put dinner on the table."

"Do you want help to speed things up?"

She shot a grateful look over her shoulder. "Would you mind?"

"That's why I'm here." He whipped off his jacket, stashed it in the hall off the bedrooms, then picked up a brush and the open paint can and began cutting in around a door. "The boys' room looks great."

"Thanks."

"Obviously, you're one of those people who can do just about anything well."

"You know me better than that."

"Oh, that's right. You're not good at stringing popcorn or accepting a compliment," he teased.

"Not when it's untrue."

"Nothing untrue about it. You're a great mother, you're teaching Hope to cook fantastic dinners in spite of her behavior toward you, you're a dynamite committee organizer, terrific office manager according to Nick and you can paint. *Plus* you're a good friend who knows how to listen with understanding and compassion. I can go on."

"Please don't. I'm a little on edge…just too much to do." She kept rolling paint as if there were no tomorrow and making lists in her head of all the things she needed to accomplish before bed tonight. Tomorrow loomed like a giant cavern of tasks that would never end.

Ben concentrated on painting. A companionable silence stretched between them.

More lists scrolled through her mind, sending her anxiety level rocketing. Okay, enough. It was time to concentrate on logic. So she was feeling a little insecure about leaving Ben's. Granted, life had gotten a whole lot better in his cozy, secure place.

Oh, come on, Alyssa. What about your struggle the past few days to keep your feelings for him to yourself?

There was that. Plus the fact that she *had* dealt with lots of problems before she'd even met Ben. And since as well, right? And she was still in one piece, and so were her boys. She'd made mistakes, but she'd done okay.

And she'd make mistakes in the future, too, but she'd be okay anyway. Besides, if she got in real trouble, Ben would be right next door. She smiled at that thought. So what was she worried about? She thought about her plans for Thanksgiving. "Will you and Hope share Thanksgiving with us?"

"Love to. You need to let me bring something."

"Are you kidding? You've been sharing your home with us for two weeks. The least you can let me do is have you over for a meal."

"Thanks. I look forward to it. And it will be nice to meet your parents."

"You can tell them about the fire."

"You haven't told them?"

"There was no point in worrying them needlessly. I figure it will be better for them to see we're all right before I tell them we were actually *in* a fire. Can you explain what happened without making it sound like total incompetence?"

"You didn't know, that's not incompetence. Anyway, your parents of all people are aware of how capable you are."

"I haven't always lived up to their expectations. Or my own, for that matter."

"I can't imagine you doing anything too shameful."

"Very disappointing would be more accurate."

"How so?"

She kept on painting. Did she really want to tell him about her past?

"You sure it won't help to talk about it?" Ben asked after a while.

"I've made mistakes. Can we just leave it at that?"

"Nope."

She blew out a breath. Why in the world had she brought up the whole thing? Where would she begin? He didn't need her life story, but she did need to frame things if he was going to understand. But what if he couldn't understand? She shook her head.

His silence hung between them until she couldn't stand it any longer.

"Fine." She cleared her throat. "You know how some people talk about being born with silver spoons in their mouths?" She glanced at him uneasily. "Well, mine was a political spoon, so to speak. My father always told me the sky was the limit for me."

"He's right. It still is."

She let out her breath in a whoosh. Maybe…if she'd been strong enough.

"Please go on. No more comments, I promise."

"Well, my parents sent me to the right schools, expected me to excel in my classes. My father was always most interested in the ones that stressed debate or public speaking or critical thinking. I tried hard to make them proud." Her voice wavered.

"I'm sure they were proud."

"Not always." She rolled paint in automatic mode, reaching for courage to admit to Ben what she hated admitting to herself. Dragging a breath, she dipped her roller in the paint pan and went back to rolling it on the wall.

Ben didn't pressure her. He just kept on painting.

She didn't want to continue. But she couldn't very well stop now, could she? "To get to the point, I...I graduated from Harvard Law School right on schedule. But I was four months pregnant with Joey."

Ben slowed his painting.

"My father was *not* pleased."

"Mothers have successful careers all the time. I'm sure he knew that."

"But I'd accepted a position with a prestigious New York law firm, which was supposed to lay the foundation for my future political endeavors. They'd promised to put me on the fast track to a partnership, provided I live, eat and breathe for them."

She rolled a swath of paint across the wall. "They'd made it very clear there would be no room for distractions like marriage or pregnancy or babies. So, of course, they withdrew their offer. I don't know if my father's ever forgiven me."

"I'm sure that's not true."

"I think he wants to. I mean he tends to listen to me more now. I just wish I'd been able to stand up to him in a better way."

"Stand up to him? You think you got pregnant on purpose?"

"I wish I knew. It took my therapist a while to get me to admit that moving to New York on my own terrified me." At least, admitting it now didn't make her stomach hurt. What Ben would now think of her did that.

"But you were in love with Joey's father, weren't you?"

"Cam was in my life for a long time. We dated off and

on, and we worked together on projects we both cared about. But marriage wasn't in our plans. He planned to save the world. I understood that. It's just that I'm not sure I knew how to let him go."

"So you married him."

"Yes. Of course, he insisted. So did my father."

"Not the best way to start a marriage, I assume."

"Could have been worse, actually. Cam was sweet. And Daddy recognized him as a worthy and ambitious man he could mentor. So Cam and I worked together on his first political campaign. I was mostly behind the scenes raising funds, which is where I'd always preferred to be. Joey was born the day Cam was elected to the state Senate."

"Sounds like quite a day."

"Joey was so tiny," she said wistfully. "Cam dived in to continue his fight to help low-income families. And I worked alongside him the way I'd done through college."

"Important work."

"It is. I acted as Cam's liaison with the Wisconsin Council on Children and Families, the Head Start Association, and WISCAP." She took a breath. "It was fascinating, challenging work I absolutely loved."

He stopped painting and turned to her. "Sounds like you found your calling."

"Maybe." She stopped painting and faced him. "But then Cam died. And Joey seemed so lost. Actually, we were both lost for a while."

"That's understandable. But you're both doing great now."

"We are. Thank you for all your help."

"I didn't do that much. Don't you dare sell yourself short."

He still had faith in her? Even when she'd admitted how weak she'd been? Drained and sad, she stood there shaking, not knowing how to stop.

Ben laid down his paintbrush and closed the gap between

them. He grasped her paint roller, laid it aside, gently took her into his arms.

She laid her head on his shoulder, drawing strength from his solid presence.

He stroked her hair the way he had the night of the fire. "You seriously need to give yourself a break. Didn't you tell me to try to think of my mistakes as experience? Hopefully, we learn. What else can you expect from yourself? Can't you see how wonderful you are?"

She gave him a self-deprecating little laugh. "Please don't tell me what you think I want to hear."

"Is that what you think I do? Tell you what you want to hear?" He lifted her chin. "You know better."

The intensity in his eyes sent her heart beating so fast that she could scarcely breathe. She reached to touch his jaw, his slight stubble tickling her fingertips.

"Alyssa," he whispered. Slipping his fingers into her hair, he drew her closer.

She focused on the look in his eyes. Her pulse beginning to dance, anticipation bubbled through her.

He turned his face to kiss her fingertips. Then he bent closer and kissed her lips.

She answered his kiss. Gentle but commanding. Filled with longing. Soft and loving and so intense. She couldn't catch her breath. She'd never felt such a kaleidoscope of emotions in her entire life.

When he broke the kiss, she wanted to protest.

"Wow," he whispered against her ear.

"More, please?" she whispered back.

He didn't waste any time granting her request.

She returned his kiss with joy, clung to him as if she'd never let him go.

"Dad!"

Alyssa stiffened, abruptly ended the kiss.

Ben gave her a confused frown.

"Hope?" Stepping away from Ben, Alyssa focused on the now-empty doorway.

Ben looked even more confused. "Hope's in school."

The girl stepped around the door frame, her pixie face contorted with anger and hurt. She glared at her father. "I tried to warn you. Why wouldn't you listen?" she yelled.

Ben stared at his daughter in shock. "Why aren't you in school?"

"The bus dropped me off, and your truck's outside the cottage. How was I to know you didn't want me here?" Fists clenched at her sides, she turned to Alyssa. "I knew you were after my dad the minute you moved in with us," she yelled. "I hope you're happy."

Alyssa shut her eyes.

"Hope," Ben said sharply.

Bursting into tears, Hope turned and ran, the front door slamming behind her seconds later.

"She doesn't mean that." He reached for Alyssa.

She laid her hand on his chest. "Go to her."

He caressed her cheek, then turned and strode out of the room to find his daughter.

Chapter Twelve

Coop charged through his kitchen, looking for Hope. He'd never seen her more upset.

"Upstairs." Lou sat at the table, sewing something with a needle and thread.

Robbie kicked and waved in his carrier nearby.

Joey looked up from his drawing. "Hi, Ben."

"Hey, Joey." He sounded as upset as Hope was. He needed to calm down, or he wouldn't get anywhere with her.

He strode through the great room, took the stairs two at a time and rapped on the giant poster of Digger covering her door. "I'm coming in." He tried to turn the knob. "You locked the door?" he asked incredulously. "Let me in."

Silence.

"Hope, let me in. If I have to get a key—"

The lock clicked.

He pushed into the room just as Hope flopped facedown onto her bedspread covered with Digger look-alikes. "Sit up. We need to have a serious talk."

She ignored him.

"I'm planning to stay right here until you look me in the eye."

She sat up, but she squeezed her eyes shut. "I don't want to look at you."

"Not proud of yourself?"

She just sat there, eyes closed, tears leaking down her cheeks.

Her tears always made him want to wrap her safely in his arms and tell her everything would be all right. And it usually was. But this situation was uncharted territory.

Covering her face with her hands, she burst into sobs.

Great. Just what he needed. He reached to comfort her.

She turned away.

He clenched his jaw against the sting of her rejection. He paced across the floor to the bookshelves loaded with books, many they'd read together. Others, they'd shared and discussed with laughter and fun.

What happened to that bond of trust and devotion? How had they gotten to this awful place? He had no idea, but he couldn't dwell on a happier time right now. Right now, he needed to man up and do the hard part of parenting. "Crying isn't going to help, kiddo."

"I'm not…not…proud of…you either," she sputtered between sobs.

He shifted his feet. "Okay. Care to explain?"

"I saw you—" she made a face "—kissing her."

He thought about how happy kissing Alyssa made him. About how much he looked forward to kissing her again. No way was he going to apologize for it. "We like each other, Hope. I'm sorry we surprised you."

"I don't want her here."

"You've made that abundantly clear with your rudeness. Don't you think you hurt her feelings every time you act like that?"

"I knew you'd take her side."

"There are no sides here."

"Are, too."

He blew out a breath. "If you feel that way, it's because she's trying and you're not."

Tears erupted all over again.

"Come on, Hope." He grabbed a couple tissues from the bedside table and handed them to her.

She took them and began mopping her face.

"She's moving out Saturday. Then it will be just you and me again. That's what you want, isn't it?"

"That doesn't mean you're going to stop seeing her, right?"

"I won't lie to you, Hope. I like her…very much. And I like being with her. Can you tell me what it is you don't like about her?"

"I don't know."

"Just give me one reason."

Her head shooting up, she looked him square in the eye. "Just because I can't tell you a reason doesn't mean I like her, does it? Stop trying to fix me, Dad."

He frowned at her. "I'm not trying to fix you."

"You try to fix everything. Mostly, it turns out good. Like our house and Digger and the newspaper and the old building in town." She sighed. "But fixing people never works."

"I don't try to fix people."

"What about my mother? And Denise? I mean, people have their own feelings. You don't get to tell anybody else how to feel. Not even me."

He scrubbed his hand over his scruffy jaw, frowned unseeingly at nothing in particular and let the words of his twelve-year-old percolate through his mind. He tried to help people. Was that so wrong?

But had he been trying to impose his feelings for Alyssa onto Hope? He wanted to deny it, but it rang too true. Is *that* why Hope resented Alyssa? It made sense, didn't it, given she couldn't come up with any reason she didn't like her? "I've never wanted to tell you how to feel. Not about Alyssa or anything else. Honest."

She focused on the floor.

"I do think it's wrong to treat people badly. Don't you?"

She nodded.

"Then why do you want to hurt Alyssa?"

"I don't want to tell you."

"Why not?"

"'Cause it will hurt your feelings."

"You think you need to protect me? That's my job."

"She's gonna leave, Dad. I know she is."

His throat felt thick. "Like your mother? And Denise?"

She still wouldn't meet his eyes.

He wanted to put his arms around her and make her insecurities go away. If only it were that simple. "Their leaving had nothing to do with you, Hope. You were the reason they dared to dream of a different life for themselves. One that included you. They just weren't able to do it, that's all."

She squinted at him as if trying to make sense of his words.

"I don't know how things will turn out with Alyssa in the long run, kiddo. But I believe she's worth taking a chance on."

She shook her head.

"Will you think about it?"

"I don't want to think about it." Flopping onto her stomach, she smothered her sobs in her bedspread. "And I don't want you to kiss her."

He flinched. "You're behaving like a child."

More crying.

Okay. She *was* a child. But she'd always been a reasonable one. Loving and kind and considerate. Easy to love. The kind you could take in your arms and talk out of a tantrum.

Too bad he didn't have any experience dealing with a kid who yelled and cried and dug in her heels when he told her to do something. If this was a taste of what teenagers were like, he wanted to go back in time in a big way. Like that was ever going to happen.

Right now, he needed to take a break. See if he could figure out what to do. But he wouldn't compromise on one thing. "I expect you to apologize to Alyssa."

"I'm not sorry. I'll never be sorry. Ever." Her words were muffled in her bedspread, but he heard them loud and clear.

"I think you need to pray about this." Chest heavy, he walked out of her room and closed the door behind him.

He needed to go over to the cottage, help Alyssa finish up painting and make sure she was okay. Striding past the guest room, he was surprised to see the door standing open. Knocking softly, he peeked inside. "Joey?"

"It's me." Relieved Ben and Hope weren't arguing anymore, Alyssa dumped a stack of clothes into one of the suitcases she'd opened on the bed.

"Lou still downstairs with the kids?" Ben moved into the room.

"She's staying to allow me to pack for a little while." She plopped another stack of clothes into the suitcase.

He closed the door behind him. "I suppose the whole house heard Hope and me?"

"Mostly Hope." The girl's "I don't want you to kiss her… I'm not sorry. I'll never be sorry. Ever" stood out in Alyssa's mind.

He crossed the room to her, his posture tense, his eyes pinched with strain. "I'm sorry."

"Who can blame her? What can possibly erase her memory of walking in on her father kissing a woman she doesn't approve of?"

"I wish she hadn't walked in when she did. But don't think for a moment I regret kissing you. I don't want you to regret it either."

She could still feel his hand in her hair, his lips on hers. She did her best to push the memory from her mind and focus on Hope. "I think she's afraid I'm displacing her. In her home. And with you."

"I've kept up her normal activities with her, done my best to reassure her…. Nothing seems to help." He clenched his jaw.

She couldn't stand seeing him so upset. She hated that she was causing a rift between him and his daughter. It couldn't go on. "I'm moving out tomorrow morning instead of waiting until Saturday."

He frowned. "Tony and his crew need tomorrow to finish up."

"I'll work around them. I can't make Hope so miserable any longer. And after seeing us kissing? It would be impossible. The poor girl is really having trouble."

"I know she is. But we didn't finish painting your bedroom."

"It's mostly done. I can finish it after I move in."

"What about the fumes with the kids?"

"I'll paint with the windows open."

"I won't be able to help you as much tomorrow. I have too many deadlines."

"I'm not your responsibility, okay? I'll ask Lou to help for a while."

He frowned. "Sounds like you have everything covered. Without my help."

"Aren't you relieved?"

He looked at her thoughtfully. "I like taking care of you and your boys."

She shook her head.

"I depend on you, too, you know," he said softly.

"But you need to focus on Hope. We all need to get our lives back on track."

He studied her as if he might try to change her mind. Instead, he reached out and moved a stray hank of hair off her cheek. "I'll put dinner on the table while you pack, and I'll carry the heavier stuff over to the cottage while you put the boys down. Deal?"

"Thank you. I'll eat later."

He narrowed his eyes. "To avoid Hope?"

"It would be miserable for all of us."

He gave a nod. "Thanks for being so understanding with her. With both of us."

"The irony is that neither of you would need understanding if not for me."

"Then good thing you're worth it."

"Are you sure about that?"

"More sure than I've been about anybody in a very long time."

She bit her lip to keep from bursting into tears. How had everything gotten so complicated?

Late-afternoon sun streaming through the window in the boys' new bedroom bleached the pale gray walls to soft white. Tony and his men had finished up by noon, and moving day was going more smoothly than Alyssa could ever have dreamed. Ben had seen to that last night. He'd handled dinner, then turned himself into a one-man moving machine.

While she had packed and organized and put the boys to bed, he'd emptied his basement of beds, new mattresses, and everything they'd salvaged from the fire or she'd brought in the U-Haul. He'd carried it all to the cottage. Then he'd helped her move suitcases and boxes of clothes she'd stored in the guest-room closet until they were both ready to drop.

Through it all, Hope had stayed in her room, and Ben had checked on her a couple of times. It was awful knowing she was the reason he and Hope were hurting so badly. Moving was the only thing she could do to help them.

Now, screwdriver in hand, she finished attaching the side rail on Robbie's maple crib and shook it to make sure it was solid.

If only she felt more solid herself. With each trip she'd made from Ben's place she'd felt less sure of herself.

But she'd moved to Rainbow Lake to be on her own, hadn't she? It was just that Ben supported her the way no one ever had. He seemed to believe she knew what she was doing. He encouraged her when she doubted herself. He made her feel that her opinions and feelings mattered. As if *she* mattered. Was that what made this separation so difficult?

Doing her best to focus on her task, she lifted the mattress into the crib, took a sheet and blankets from the changing table and began making the bed.

Joey's attitude about the move certainly didn't help. She'd been trying to prepare him. But when she'd told him they were leaving this morning, he'd launched a major tantrum, and no amount of assurance that they'd be living right next door to Ben had consoled him.

Thankfully, he'd taken a long nap at Ben's this afternoon. And since Ben had come home from work early, Joey had been following him and his dog around like a lost puppy. What if he regressed into the timid, little boy he'd become when Cam died?

Trying to shake off her worry, she rummaged in the changing table drawer for Robbie's Pooh Bear mobile. She located it, hung it on the crib and switched on the music box. Anticipating Robbie's reaction to the cheerful tune made her feel better.

Once she was all moved in, she'd enjoy fixing up the place and organizing it to fit her little family's needs. It would give her a sense of accomplishment. And she had only a few days before her parents would be here for Thanksgiving. She had too much to do to miss Ben, right?

With that thought spurring her into action, she glanced at the empty bookshelf. Displaying some of Joey's toys would surprise him and might help him settle in. She opened the suitcase he'd helped her pack full of toys.

The only ones left in the case were Robbie's. What had Joey done with his things? She walked to the kitchen to find out.

Sitting in his carrier on the floor, Robbie kicked and waved his arms and jabbered at Digger lying near him. Ben and Joey knelt beside Gram's upside-down table, Ben's dark head and Joey's blond one bent over the legs.

A perfect picture. Too bad she'd misplaced her phone camera earlier in the day and been unable to locate it yet. "What's the problem?"

"It wiggles, but we can fix it," Joey said confidently. "Can't we, Ben?"

"Sure can." Ben looked up at her, his dark eyes so intense she melted before she had enough sense to focus on the table. Oh yeah, moving into her own place made sense. All she had to do was to figure out how to stop missing him. Of course, he *would* still be right next door.

He took a power tool from his tool belt and handed it to Joey. "This is called a drill. You can look at it, but you need to be very careful with it, okay?"

Joey gave him a serious nod.

Ben glanced up at Alyssa. "The screws stripped the brittle wood, but a brace should take care of it." He rummaged in the toolbox beside him, took out screws and widgets and laid them beside the table leg.

She focused on her son. "Your toys are missing from the big suitcase we packed. Do you know what happened to them?"

Joey curiously examined Ben's power drill. "My toys want to live at Ben's house."

Why wasn't she surprised? "Won't you miss them? Because you will be living here with Robbie and me."

Putting on a serious pout, he glowered at her. "I'm going to live with Ben and Digger and Hope."

"Can't happen, buddy."

"Why?"

"Because Hope goes to school all day, and I go to work." Ben took his drill from Joey and used it on the table, the loud buzz startling Robbie.

He just looked around, as if he was getting used to hearing unfamiliar sounds.

Ben slipped the drill back in his tool belt.

"I can take care of Digger while you're gone," Joey said.

"Robbie will miss you," Alyssa said. "I'll miss you, too. What will I do without my helper?"

Joey looked as if he was ready to cry. He stood and wrapped his arms around Ben's neck. "I love you, Ben."

Ben folded his arms around her son. "I love you, too, buddy."

Tears stung her eyes. Another perfect picture she wasn't capturing.

"It's scary here," Joey said into Ben's neck.

Was he afraid there would be another fire? "We'll be safe now, honey. Tony fixed the chimney for the fireplace."

"It's good as new," Ben pointed out.

Joey pulled back to look at Ben. "What if robbers come?"

"We don't have robbers around here."

"Uh-huh. A boy stole Hope's pencil case out of her backpack on her school bus."

"I didn't know that," Ben said. "But nobody on Rainbow Lake has ever had their house robbed, so there's no reason for you to worry."

"Digger needs me to feed him."

Ben ruffled the boy's hair. "Hope will fill in for you. Digger loves her, too, remember?"

"Yeah." Joey's lip quivered. "Digger's gonna forget me."

"Never. How can he forget you? Besides, you can visit him whenever your mommy says you can."

Joey sighed. "Can you stay with us tonight, Ben?"

"No, buddy, I can't. I need to stay with Hope. You know that."

"Then can I sleep with you? I don't take much room."

"God will keep you safe in your new house just like He did at mine."

"God don't know I moved."

"Sure, He does. God knows everything."

Joey looked at Ben, eyes wide. "Do you promise you won't go live in heaven, too?"

She bit her lip. How was she going to get him past this?

"I promise I'm staying right next door." Throwing a concerned look her way, Ben climbed to his feet. "I need my flashlight, Joey. Do you know where you left it when you played with it earlier?"

Joey frowned, obviously trying to remember what he'd done with the flashlight. Then he took off for the living room.

"I have an idea I think could help him adjust." Ben kept his voice low.

"Anything."

"How do you feel about Digger staying the night?"

"Oh. Joey would be thrilled. But he'll probably expect the dog to stay every night."

"I'll make it very clear we're loaning out Digger only for Joey's first night in his new place."

"It's a good idea. He'll be so excited about the dog staying, maybe he'll sail right past his fears."

Or maybe not. But at least, it was worth a try.

Chapter Thirteen

Sunday morning, Coop drove a sullen, uncommunicative girl masquerading as his daughter to church. Because this wasn't Hope's Sunday to volunteer in the nursery, he escorted her into the pew and sat down beside Alyssa and Robbie. But being close to Alyssa only reminded him how much he missed her.

Now, he strode down the hall headed for the fellowship room. Maybe coffee would clear his mind. Hope had scuttled off to Sunday school. And concerned about Joey depending on Coop too much, Alyssa had insisted on getting the boy from the nursery without his help. He didn't want to make it harder for Joey. Surely, Alyssa knew that. But he loved her boys, and he enjoyed helping her with them.

He jammed his hands into his pockets. Besides, he liked her to need him. He needed *her*. He needed the boys. And he needed the wonderful life he'd had a taste of while they'd lived with him.

But he needed to put Hope first. And he did. It was just that in spite of Hope's insecurities, he literally ached to have Alyssa and the boys in his home where he could make sure they were all right. How sane was that?

"Morning, Coop." Tony fell into step beside him.

Coop glanced around for Maggie. "Where's your better half?"

"Choir meeting today. Alyssa and the boys getting settled into her cottage?"

Coop nodded.

"Enjoying your peace and quiet?"

"I don't know what to do with myself."

"Your two families seem like a good fit." Tony gave him an encouraging look. "You thinking about pursuing that idea?"

Coop didn't want to get into it.

Tony narrowed his eyes. "Touchy subject?"

"Afraid so."

"How so?"

Coop shook his head. "I need coffee." He didn't want to be rude, but he wanted even less to talk about the situation. Last night during supper, he'd mentioned he couldn't get used to the quiet, and Hope had huffed off to her room where she'd holed up for the remainder of the evening. Truth was, he didn't want to get used to the quiet. He walked over to the table, grabbed a cup and flipped the spigot on the urn to fill it.

"Ben!" Joey came running full tilt.

Coop set his cup down just in time to scoop the boy up, his familiar, warm-boy scent comforting. "How was nursery this morning?"

"We played music chairs."

"Sounds fun."

Alyssa, with Robbie in her arms, glided across the room toward them looking beautiful in gray-and-pink silk.

Coop did all he could do not to break into song. Instead, he dragged a breath and attempted to act normal. Even when just standing beside her made him feel like the most fortunate man on planet Earth. Even if she did live next door now. Even if she didn't want to depend on him. Or want Joey depending on him either. Even when his own daughter was lost in her insecurities and struggling to make sense of them.

None of it kept him from missing Alyssa's companionship and the little womanly things she did to help make his house a home. Things like the herbs she'd planted in containers and arranged on a tray by the kitchen window. And the lamp she'd moved near the chair he read in. And the colorful orb she'd hung in the skylight to reflect the sun's rays across the kitchen in the morning.

He'd never planned on missing the sound of her voice when she sang to her baby. Or the fresh, exotic scent that followed her. Or the way she looked up when he entered a room as if sensing his presence.

Sure, he'd fallen in love the first time he'd laid eyes on Hope. But he was thirty-four years old, and he was learning firsthand what falling in love with a woman felt like. Just having Alyssa near him was exhilarating, uplifting, life-altering, and he never wanted it to end.

"Ben, will you help me get a choclit doughnut, please?"

Coop did his best to come down from the clouds long enough to get Joey a doughnut, set him up at the child's table to eat it and stand guard in case the boy needed him.

Moving to stand beside him, Alyssa looked at Joey. Smiled. "Thanks."

"My pleasure." Gazing into her deep blue eyes, he didn't know what to say. She probably wasn't ready to hear how he felt anyway.

But he was definitely getting the feeling he'd found the woman he never wanted to live without.

Seeing nothing going on at Ben's house, Alyssa stepped back from the cottage window and peered intently at the sunny gold curtains she'd just hung in the living room. Did one seem a tad crooked? How had that happened when she'd measured so carefully? She couldn't even get straight seams right? Who knew simple sewing was so difficult?

Sighing, she decided to see how much it bothered her to live with imperfect curtains. She focused on the newly shampooed floral sofa Fred's thrift store had delivered yesterday. Sighed. Not the right vibe for cottage chic, but she'd live with it until she had time to sharpen her sewing skills. She really wanted to make her own slipcover like she'd done with Gram when she was a girl.

She settled at the kitchen table to move her lampshade project to the next stage, then realized the glue hadn't dried enough to work on it. So she grabbed the bottle of furniture oil Lou had recommended she use. Humming a hymn from church this morning, she settled on the floor and rubbed oil on the old trunk–turned–coffee table.

She finished polishing the trunk, the rocking chair she'd found at Slim's Treasures last week and every stick of furniture in the cottage. Except the boys' room, because they were still napping.

Wasn't it about time for them to wake up? She checked the clock above the sink. Hmm. It wasn't as late as she'd thought.

It was too quiet when the boys napped. Too lonely after they went to bed in the evenings. She walked into the living room and looked out the window again. Still nothing going on over there. Were they reading or on their computers or napping? But they never napped. Maybe they'd gone someplace?

Ben had looked so handsome sitting beside her in church this morning in a medium blue sweater and khakis. She'd struggled to keep her eyes off him. But didn't he always look handsome?

Hope, on the other hand, had looked awful, her face puffy

as if she'd been crying quite a bit. Had she and Ben been talking, or was Hope still hiding out in her room?

In either case, their demeanors said they weren't happy with each other. And it was her fault, of course.

She groaned, realizing how pathetic she was. Why couldn't she keep busy enough to stop missing them and the active household they'd shared? Making herself leave the window, she marched into the kitchen, took out baking paraphernalia and Gram's cookbook and whipped up a double batch of chocolate oatmeal cookies.

"I'm not tired anymore, Mommy. Please can I visit Ben and Hope and Digger now?" Joey stood just inside the kitchen, hair sleep-tousled, eyes pleading.

He looked so forlorn and miserable she wanted to cry. "No, honey. It's so quiet over there, I don't even think they're home." The oven timer pinged. She took the last cookie sheet from the oven. "I made chocolate oatmeal cookies. Would you like one with milk?"

"I'm not hungry." He turned and trudged out of the room.

"Where are you going?"

"To sleep with Robbie."

Now, she was getting worried. "How would you like to take a ride?"

"To see Ben and Hope and Digger?" He brightened.

"No." She thought a moment. "Let's go visit Mr. Krentz."

"The man that pulled our car out of the snow with his tractor?"

"That's the one. Do you want to help me pack up some cookies for him?"

He nodded.

Forty minutes later, Zebadiah Krentz grumpily opened his door to Alyssa's knock. "Stuck again?"

"I baked cookies," Alyssa said. "So we brought you some."

Zebadiah didn't lose his frown, but he did step back to allow them to come inside.

Joey handed the plastic container to the old man.

He grunted. "What kind?"

"Choclit oatmeal," Joey answered. "They taste real good."

"You make them?"

Joey shook his head. "Mommy cooked 'em when Robbie and me were asleep."

"Go ahead, try one," Alyssa encouraged.

He set the container on the table, opened the lid and took out a cookie. "Want one, Joseph?"

"My tummy's full."

"These are for you," Alyssa explained. "I hope you like them."

Zebadiah replaced the cover, took a bite of cookie. He looked Alyssa straight in the eye. "A pie. Now, cookies. Do I look like I need fattening up?"

"I figured feeding your sweet tooth couldn't hurt. When was the last time you baked for yourself?"

He frowned. "Never. The last time I had anything home baked was probably something your gramma Emma gave me."

Alyssa had guessed right. "I used her recipe for these cookies."

"Hmm. Never would have guessed that. These are pretty good."

"Not as good as Gram's, though, right?"

He shook his head. "Emma was a good cook. But she never did get the hang of baking."

His words shocked her. "Are you kidding me?"

He narrowed his eyes. "I don't know you well enough to do that."

"I loved Gram's cookies."

"You were a kid. You probably loved anything sweet."

She frowned. She thought about Joey's indiscriminate taste for sweet things. Did Zebadiah have a point? But it didn't really matter because she'd never believe Gram's baking was anything but amazing. "You said you'd like to see my father again. My parents are coming to Rainbow Lake to celebrate Thanksgiving with us at the cottage. If you'll join us, I'll have my father pick you up."

He finished off his cookie and pointed at her. "Trying to lure me out into the world, I take it."

"Only to Gram's little cottage. You used to go there, right?"

"Went to see *her*. Doesn't mean I need to go there anymore. Joseph can come here if he wants to see me."

"Then I'll send Thanksgiving dinner over with him."

"You cook as well as you bake?"

"Since I took a cooking class, I haven't had any complaints. I've never roasted a turkey before, though, so I'll depend on you to give me your honest opinion."

"It's the only kind worth giving."

She thought about his words. She could count on Zebadiah to speak his mind, and he often had important things to say. "How did you get so wise?"

He narrowed his eyes as if considering her question. "Wisdom comes from God. You think maybe He's finally getting through?"

"I think you're onto something."

"You go to church?"

"I have been lately. If you'd like to go, I'll pick you up."

"What makes you think I need to go to church to find Him?"

"I don't think that. I haven't gone to church much. Especially not since my husband's funeral."

"Why did you go back?"

Good question. Why had she gone back? "Ben Cooper

invited me to go with his daughter and him. And I began working there. The day care for my boys is there. And there's something inspiring about worshipping with others. Do you think that's one reason Jesus said He'd be wherever two or more are gathered in His name?"

"You're asking the wrong man, missy. I prefer private talks. No distractions. No fuss. No bother. Never had much use for a lot of people. I used to go to church 'cause Viola liked to go. Then your grandmother said she liked having company when she went, so I'd go with her."

"You and Gram were really good friends, weren't you?"

"We watched out for each other." He got a funny look on his face. "Even helped each other out a few times when we got ourselves in trouble."

Alyssa perked up at that. "What kind of trouble?"

"You think I'm going to tattle on your grandmother?"

She laughed. "I'm curious."

"Well, you're just going to have to live with it." He shuffled over to the door. "Young Cooper brought me a new generator the other day. Says the old one can't be fixed. Think I can trust him?"

"Absolutely. I've never met a more trustworthy man."

"I thought so. I appreciate the cookies."

Apparently, he was dismissing her. She sighed. She sure wasn't looking forward to another long, lonely evening once she put the boys to bed.

"The turkey smells and looks absolutely delicious, dear."

"Thanks, Mother." Alyssa set the roaster containing the beautifully browned turkey on the cutting board with a thud. She slipped the sheet of rolls into the oven and glanced through the window at the sparkling new landscape dusted with last night's snow.

Ben would be arriving soon, and she couldn't keep her

excitement at bay. She'd seen him only briefly when he'd dropped off a box of their items he'd found around his house. She assumed he would have told her if he'd had any breakthroughs with Hope, so she hadn't asked. Would Hope come with him?

She didn't know what to expect where Hope was concerned. But she'd missed them both so much, even if she had been terribly busy getting settled and preparing for Thanksgiving and the fund-raiser.

At least Ben would be here today. And he'd meet her parents who'd arrived last night. It was so good to see them. They'd been genuinely thrilled to see the boys again. They'd been trying to win Robbie over and playing nonstop with Joey ever since.

Right now, Daddy was teaching Joey how to play checkers in the living room while she and her mother pulled the meal together. Hopefully, Robbie would nap until they'd finished eating.

She was mashing potatoes when a knock on the front door sent the masher flying from her hand, spraying potatoes everywhere.

She began cleaning them off herself and the counter, wall and floor around her. Thankfully, the tablecloth and set table were far enough away to be missed. She'd wanted to greet Ben at the door and introduce him to her parents, but that was before cleaning up potatoes demanded her attention.

"Welcome." Her father's voice boomed from the other room.

Ben's deep voice mingled with Hope's and Joey's excited ones. Hope had come after all. Alyssa whipped off her apron, stashed it in a nearby cupboard and smoothed her hair.

Her mother chuckled. "I can't wait to meet him."

"He's…" She swallowed, too many superlatives crowding her mind to choose just one or two. Pressing her hands to her hot cheeks, she shook her head.

"I've never seen you like this."

"I've never felt like this."

"Never?"

She met her mother's questioning gaze. "Cam and I worked together for a long time. We were a team. But this... this is magic." She shook her head. "Not that it can go anywhere."

"How well can you really know him in such a short time?"

"I know he's a kind, caring, wonderful man," Alyssa defended. "But I'm doing my best to—"

"Your best smells fantastic." Ben's voice sent shivers through her.

She turned to face him.

He filled the doorway, a glass vase of pink roses in one hand, a bottle of sparkling cider in the other. He gave her the smile that made her knees go weak. "You look wonderful."

All she could do was answer his smile. She remembered they weren't alone. "Mother, meet Ben Cooper," she said proudly.

"So nice to meet you, Ben." Her mother took the bottle, then shook his hand.

"A real pleasure, Mrs. Bradley." He flashed *the* smile.

Her mother responded the way any woman would.

Hiding a little smile, Alyssa gave the simmering gravy a quick stir before it could scorch, then turned back to Ben.

"These are for you." He stepped toward her.

She floated over to take the flowers from him. "Thank you. They're so beautiful." She quickly replaced the fall centerpiece on the table with his gorgeous roses and stood back to admire. "Pink is my favorite."

"I remember." He met her eyes. "You were very specific about shades of pink the day we painted."

The day…they'd kissed. She should be doing something, but she couldn't seem to recall what it was.

"The gravy, dear."

Oh, yes. She flew to the stove to save the gravy.

"Ben, we're very grateful to you for helping Alyssa and the boys escape the fire and for giving them a place to stay. We'd like to repay you in some way."

"Mother." Suddenly feeling like an adolescent with her parent riding interference, Alyssa gave her mother an embarrassed glance.

"It wasn't a one-way street, Mrs. Bradley. Alyssa contributed more than my daughter and I did. We miss her and the boys every day." He moved behind her, resting his hand briefly at her waist. "You okay?" he asked close to her ear.

She gave him a private smile when what she wanted to do was to step into his arms. But not with her mother watching. And Hope was in the living room. It was just that she'd missed him even more than she'd realized. "I'm glad Hope came with you."

He seemed to flinch.

Uh-oh. He'd probably insisted she come.

"I'll open the cider," he suggested.

"Thanks." She pointed. "Glasses are in the cupboard over the fridge."

He set to work.

She concentrated on scooping stuffing out of the bird. When she'd finished, she carried the turkey to the table to join the side dishes. "Mother, the rolls need to come out of the oven. Will you please fill the bread basket? Ben, will you tell everybody it's time to eat?"

When people were settled, Alyssa looked at the special group sitting around Gram's old table, her heart threatening to burst with love. "Thank you for sharing Thanksgiving with us in our new home. It means the world to me to have you all here. Ben, would you say grace?"

Her parents stifled their surprise as they bowed their heads.

"Good and merciful Lord," Ben began, "we thank You for continuing to heal this family from the loss of their beloved mother and grandmother and their husband, father, son-in-law. We ask Your blessing on this delicious food Alyssa has prepared for us. And we thank You for the privilege of sharing it together in the home she has so lovingly provided. In Jesus's name we pray. Amen."

Ben's face blurred through Alyssa's tears. Only *he* would be thoughtful enough to pray that prayer. "Thank you," she whispered.

"A beautiful prayer, Ben," Mother said.

"Well done, Cooper." Her father cleared his throat, picked up the carving knife and fork and set to work on the turkey.

"Please, pass whatever's near you." Alyssa spooned mashed potatoes onto Joey's and her plates, then passed the bowl to a disgruntled-looking Hope. Alyssa smiled. "Here you go, Hope. I'm glad you came."

A little frown crossed the girl's features as she took the bowl.

Alyssa hated that Hope was still so unhappy. If only there was something she could do to help.

When Alyssa's father finished carving the turkey, he handed the platter to her and turned to Ben. "So what's your take on the politics of this great nation of ours?"

"We're having a family dinner, Joe," her mother reminded.

Thanks, Mom. Alyssa shot an empathetic look at Ben. He didn't need Daddy's inquisition. He would handle himself brilliantly, but still, at the Thanksgiving table? *Really, Daddy?*

"I'm interested in learning about our guest," her father pointed out. "Aren't you?"

"Of course I am," Mother returned. "But I want to get to know *him,* not his politics."

"A man's politics say a lot about the man," her father stated unequivocally.

"Ben's a man," Joey piped up.

Ben grinned at Joey. "That's right, buddy."

Joey looked proud. "His dog's name is Digger. We play ball. And Hope's Ben's girl. She helps me make snow people. And she's teaching me a computer game, too, Grampa."

Daddy nodded. "That's nice, Joey."

"Hope knows a lot."

"I'm sure she does, dear," Mother interjected. "What kind of computer game are you teaching him, Hope?"

Hope shot a narrow-eyed look at Ben, then looked back to Alyssa's mother. "It teaches little kids how to add and subtract."

Good work, Hope. The educational merits of a game are important to Mother.

"It has amimals," Joey explained. "All kinds of amimals. Even cows."

Mother smiled. "Maybe you can show me the game later?"

Joey turned to Hope. "Can we show my grandma?"

"I guess."

Not enthusiastic, but at least she'd agreed. Her soft spot for Joey seemed to be intact, and he was drawing her out of her shell a little whether she liked it or not. Alyssa shot a quick look at Ben.

He gave her a little smile. "Delicious meal."

She smiled back. "I'm glad you like it."

"He's right, Lissa," Daddy said. "Wonderful meal."

"Thanks, Daddy."

"Can we eat punkin pie now?" Joey asked.

Alyssa looked at the untouched food on his plate. "Eat some of your turkey first."

"I'll race you," Hope challenged.

Joey shook his head. "My tummy hurts."

"Then you can't eat pie." Hope gave him a sober look.

"Can, too."

Alyssa loved hearing their interchanges again. If only Hope and Ben could find their way back to their terrific relationship, now that Alyssa was no longer underfoot.

"Let's put some gravy on that turkey, Joey." Alyssa's father reached for the boy's plate and doused gravy over everything.

Joey tried it tentatively, then dug in.

A coo came over the monitor speaker.

"Uh-oh," Alyssa said. "Somebody's awake."

"We'll clean up the kitchen while you take care of him," her mother suggested. "Then we'll have room for pie later."

Everybody nodded, even Joey who was eating nearly everything on his plate that her father had smothered with gravy.

"You kids are excused," Ben said. "I think Joey needs a snow family in his yard, don't you, Hope?"

"Sure." Hope looked relieved.

Alyssa pushed back her chair and stood. She'd actually pulled everything together to host the family dinner in Gram's little cottage that she'd dreamed of through this difficult year. Her parents had to see she was getting back on her feet, right?

Chapter Fourteen

Sidestepping Alyssa's mother in the tiny kitchen, Coop ran the sink full of hot water and started washing dishes while Alyssa took care of Robbie in the boys' bedroom.

Things had gone better with Hope than he feared they might. Alyssa seemed pleased he'd brought her. Good thing he'd weathered Hope's arguments and made her come with him.

"Why didn't Alyssa have a dishwasher installed?" Mrs. Bradley continued putting leftovers into plastic containers and storing them in the fridge. She'd already put together a care package for Zebadiah and sent it off with the senator.

"The septic system can't handle a dishwasher," Coop explained. "And new septic systems are very expensive."

"Why in the world doesn't she cash our monthly checks if she needs money?" Sounding upset, Mrs. Bradley put her hand to her forehead. "I'm sorry. I'm just so worried about her."

Monthly checks? He could imagine how well *that* went over with Alyssa. "She wants to make it on her own."

"That's just it. She won't accept our help when she clearly needs it. And who really knows *how* she's doing when she lives so far away?"

Couldn't Mrs. Bradley see Alyssa was doing great? Seemed to be enough parent–child communication problems to go around. He put a lot of energy into scrubbing and went back to thinking about Hope. At least she'd tried with Joey. But even though she was living in the same house with him, *his* Hope had gone missing, and he didn't know how to get her back. Not that he'd ever throw in the towel, no matter how determined she was to shut him out or how rude she behaved. It was time she realized that. He scrubbed a little harder.

"Joey and your daughter really enjoy each other, don't they?" Mrs. Bradley asked.

"They hit it off right away."

"Kind of like you and Alyssa did?"

He stopped scrubbing and glanced at her.

She gave him a little smile.

What had Alyssa told her? Not knowing just how to answer her question, he played it safe and didn't say anything.

"Does Hope approve?"

Apparently, Mrs. Bradley didn't miss a thing. "She's trying to figure things out."

"Is her mother around?"

"She died when Hope was two."

"I'm sorry to hear that. So it's just been you and your daughter all these years?"

He nodded.

"Ah. She's used to having you all to herself."

"Any advice?"

"Be patient. Take it slow." Mrs. Bradley looked thoughtful. "Things have a way of working themselves out if you give them time."

"I appreciate that." Maybe she was right. Hope had to realize she was wrong about Alyssa sooner or later, didn't she? He went back to scrubbing dishes. But what was he going to do until Hope figured it out? What if she didn't? Not only did he miss his daughter, but also Alyssa's absence in his life was like a wound he didn't know how to heal. It couldn't go on like this.

The front door slammed, and Senator Bradley strode into the kitchen, picked up a towel and began drying dishes. "Well, that trip was a complete waste of time."

"What happened?" With surprise written on her face, Mrs. Bradley stood in front of the open refrigerator door, a container of food in each hand.

"Rude old fool took the food, told me I should be proud of my daughter and closed the door in my face."

"That's odd," Mrs. Bradley said.

"He usually doesn't even open the door," Coop explained. "He's been a recluse since before I moved here. I met him only recently when Alyssa introduced us."

Senator Bradley shook his head. "What happened to him?"

"Consensus seems to blame his wife's death."

The senator shook his head. "Can't be easy for any man."

"No," Coop agreed even though he'd never had a wife.

"So tell me about the newspaper business, Ben."

Coop looked the senator in the eye and launched into one of his favorite topics.

After everybody enjoyed a slice of pumpkin pie with whipped cream, Hope went home and Alyssa put Joey down for a nap.

She asked Ben to join her and her parents in the living room. It might be a little uncomfortable, but she wasn't ready for him to leave.

"It certainly is more cheerful in here than it was last spring when we came for your grandmother's funeral," Mother said.

Alyssa rocked Robbie in the old rocking chair, wanting to believe Mother was referring to the entire cottage and not just the colorful couch.

"It looks great." Ben gave her a little smile.

"Thanks."

"Not sure where you found the time, but you've transformed the place," Ben said.

"Yes…well, the cottage is very…quaint," her father said. "And you have happy memories at Rainbow Lake, so I can see why hosting Thanksgiving here appealed to you."

Alyssa smiled. "Thank you for understanding, Daddy."

He frowned as if he had something on his mind. "Lyle Jennings believes your law background and your experience at the state level is a perfect background to make you an invaluable asset on his national committee to eliminate poverty in this country."

"Are you serious?" She couldn't stop her mind from racing at the opportunity to help countless people.

"Lyle asked me to find out if you're interested."

"Of course I'm interested. Presenting Cam's and my views to Representative Jennings's influential committee sounds wonderful."

"He sent an offer for you to look at."

"An offer?"

"He's offering you a position on the committee, Lissa. And I happen to know the financial package that goes with it will be more than adequate for you to maintain the lifestyle you've become accustomed to over the years."

She frowned. "I wish you would have talked to me before you asked him to offer me a position."

"Your unique experience at the state level can be extremely important to them. Lyle recognizes that."

"Thank you for your confidence, Daddy. But that would require my moving to Washington."

"It would give your mother and me the opportunity to be the doting grandparents we want to be."

"Friends are moving from a perfect condo for you and the children," Mrs. Bradley said matter-of-factly. "If you decide to come to Washington, of course."

Hadn't she expected them to use the "move to Washington" argument? "I'm not moving, Mother. I love Gram's cottage."

Ben shot her a supportive smile.

"You made it clear when Cam died that you want to maintain your independence," Senator Bradley asserted. "That's why we put a deposit on the condo to prevent somebody else from snatching it up if you accept Jennings's offer."

"I'm sorry you went to the trouble, Daddy."

"I can't see you and the boys living in these conditions very long." Daddy glanced around the room as if he found it distasteful.

No accounting for taste. "We're very comfortable here."

"You don't even have a dishwasher," Mrs. Bradley objected.

"Which makes us more environmentally friendly," Alyssa countered.

"You need to think about your children." Her father's voice rose in the rhetorical tone he used to convince anybody with an opposing view to adopt his way of thinking. "It's extremely important you raise them to fill their potential."

Shifting in his chair, Ben straightened as if gearing up to jump into the fray.

"My boys are still babies." She wrapped Robbie closer. "The last thing they need is pressure to fill their potential."

"If you don't provide them with the necessary tools as they grow up, you'll essentially be crippling them," her father declared.

"Alyssa is a wonderful mother," Ben said flatly. "To suggest she's crippling her children in any way is not only untrue, it's just plain wrong."

Her father turned to Ben. "I appreciate your coming to my daughter's defense. It speaks highly of your regard for her. I, too, want only what's best for my daughter and what will make her happy. But I expect her to examine her motives and be able to give me a well-thought-out argument for whatever that is."

Ben scowled. "With all due respect, sir, she's your daughter, as well as a talented and accomplished woman and mother. Doesn't she deserve your understanding and support without arguing for it?"

"She knows she has my support." Daddy narrowed his eyes as if ready to draw blood. "I'm sure she knows she has yours, too."

Why were they talking about her as if she wasn't in the room? "Daddy, I'll write a letter to thank Representative Jennings for his consideration. But I can't go to Washington."

"You haven't even read his offer."

"I don't need to. I love my boys with all my heart. And I can't be the mother I want to be and do justice to a position that will take over my life."

"But that's the beauty of serving on Jennings's committee. He's a family man. He knows the time commitment a family takes. You'll need to attend the meetings, but you can devote as much time as you can beyond that. It will fill out your résumé while you're raising the boys."

"I've never seen you approach anything with less than your all. I can't either, Daddy. And I want to invest my all in raising my boys."

Her father shook his head impatiently.

"We don't need an answer now, do we, Joe?" Mother asked diplomatically. "Come to Washington, dear. Play 'what-if?' Talk to Representative Jennings. Look at the condo. Check out schools. What harm could it do?"

"Excellent suggestion." Her father raised his hand to stop Alyssa's objection. "It will give you the chance to gather information you need to make an informed decision. You have too much curiosity and intelligence to make an uninformed one."

Ben sat silent and stone-faced.

She'd thought it might get uncomfortable, but not this bad. "I put a lot of thought into moving here, Daddy. I have a job I like, and it fits in beautifully with being a full-time mom. We found the most fantastic day-care center for a few hours a week. Joey loves it, and it's right down the hall from my office, so I can nurse Robbie. I'm even getting involved with the church—"

"So things at Rainbow Lake are giving you the challenge you need right now," her father conceded. "But once you get Rainbow Lake out of your system, what then?"

"Out of my system? I'm not a teenager anymore, Daddy. You can't live my life for me. I need to live it for myself and my boys. I need to stand on my own."

Her father narrowed his eyes. "Is that what you think you're doing, Lissa? Why you're not cashing our checks?"

"Yes, it is. I've asked you before to please instruct your accountant to stop sending them."

"I hope you're wise enough to stash them away for a time when you need them."

"Actually, I tear them up."

He shook his head. "You're as bad as your grandmother about accepting help."

That got her attention. "Thank you." She narrowed her eyes. "I suppose you wanted her to move to Washington, too."

"She wouldn't even consider it. Wouldn't take a dime,

even sold her cottage to Zebadiah Krentz to pay off a loan. Her records showed she finished buying it back about a year before she died."

Zebadiah? He'd said he and Gram had helped each other when they'd gotten in trouble. Is *that* what he meant?

"I wanted to make her life better," her father said sadly.

"But it wasn't the independent life she wanted, Daddy. Can't you understand that?"

"You talk a good game about being your own woman like your grandmother. But you're kidding yourself. In her case, that apparently didn't apply to Zebadiah. With you, it doesn't appear to apply to Ben. Haven't you been relying on him ever since you came to Rainbow Lake?"

She stared at her father. Had she been fooling herself to think she was learning to stand on her own? Wasn't relying on Ben exactly what she'd been doing ever since she moved here? Even moving back to the cottage, she'd known he would be right next door if she needed him. She shot Ben a questioning look.

He met her gaze. "You haven't been relying on me or anybody else to make your decisions or run your life."

She frowned. Confused. Unsure.

"You haven't." He turned to her father. "The only thing I did was to give her and the boys a place to live while the cottage was being repaired and winterized."

She shook her head. "I've relied on you for a lot more than that," she said sadly. "If I hadn't, I wouldn't need your reassurance."

Coop flinched at the certainty in her voice, not even sure what it meant. Or how to answer her. "Alyssa?"

She pressed her fingers to her forehead and shook her head.

He did his best to understand what was happening. What

had he missed? She'd been as glad to see him as he was to see her when he'd arrived. He was sure of it. She'd included him and Hope as if they were part of the family, even with Hope's attitude. She'd even invited him to stay to visit with her parents as if she wasn't any more ready for him to leave than he was.

Then what was going on? One remark from her father about her not standing on her own as she claimed, and suddenly, she was shutting down? Leaving him on the outside looking in? He didn't get it.

He'd been living an independent life for longer than he cared to remember. It was definitely overrated. He liked relying on her. Loved knowing she relied on him for a few things. At least, she had when she'd lived in his house.

But she didn't live at his place anymore, did she? He was on her turf now, knee-deep in her relationship with her parents. A relationship she'd told him about, and he'd thought he understood.

Obviously, he'd been wrong. He needed to get out of here so she could deal with them. He stood. "I need to check on Hope." Striding across the room, he grabbed his jacket from the coat tree and walked out the door.

Fresh, cold air slapping him in the face, he jogged for home.

An enthusiastic Digger greeted him, but the rest of the house was quiet. He walked upstairs, knocked on Hope's closed door.

"What?"

He opened her door. "You okay?"

"I guess so." Lying on her bed, she looked up from her book. "What happened?"

"Nothing."

"You look upset."

He shook his head, unwilling to admit his concerns to his

daughter. They'd probably make her happy. It wasn't as if he didn't bring his own problems into the mix with Alyssa, was it? "Tired, that's all. Probably too much turkey." Realizing he was exhausted, he turned and left.

A few minutes later, he lay across his bed, his arm flung over his eyes, trying to stop the flurry of thoughts and fears badgering him. Would Hope ever open her mind to Alyssa? And even if she did, would Alyssa someday need him like he needed her? Would she ever let him protect her and take care of her?

Sure, she'd refused the job offer in Washington the senator brought with him. But Coop had seen the excitement in her eyes when her father brought it up. The same excitement he'd seen when she'd told him about her work in Madison with her state senator husband.

A woman like Alyssa could do anything she wanted. Anywhere in the world. Nobody knew better than he did how talented she was. Did he really expect her to choose to permanently settle down in northern Wisconsin?

He'd made that choice, and he'd never regretted the way things were turning out. Well, except for never dating. But he hadn't really wanted to date…until now. The toughest thing to swallow was that in the grand scheme of things, Alyssa didn't need him. Didn't want to need him.

Digger started barking and raced down the stairs.

He doubted Hope would trouble herself to see what the dog was barking about. He dragged himself off the bed and strode to find out what was going on. Halfway across the kitchen, he spied Digger standing at the back door, wagging his tail and most of his body as if waiting to greet one of his best friends in the world.

"Sit, Dig." Coop opened the door.

Alyssa stood on the step, looking unsure and worried.

He had no idea why she was here, but he didn't care. He'd never been more glad to see anybody in his entire life. "Well, hello."

Seeing Ben set off a zillion butterflies inside Alyssa. She desperately wanted to throw her arms around his neck and hug him. But she wasn't here for a hug. "Funny how much I've missed that noisy dog."

"Come in."

"Can we take Digger for a walk instead?"

"Hope's in her room."

Where Hope was didn't matter at the moment. Alyssa couldn't be in an enclosed space with him. She needed to think straight. "I need some fresh air, okay?"

"Sure." Ben grabbed his jacket off its hook, held the door to allow the dog outside and followed.

Digger wriggled himself practically inside out for her attention.

"Good boy." She knelt in the snow to pet him and scratch behind his ears where he especially loved it.

"Fortunate dog," Ben murmured.

She pretended not to hear. With a final pat, she stood and Digger bounded off.

Ben started to reach for her, then changed his mind.

In his arms was exactly where she wanted to be. But a shiver reminded her why she was here.

"Cold?"

"A little. Let's walk to stay warm."

He fell into step beside her, their breaths sending steam into the dusk. "What's bothering you?"

"My feelings for you," she said honestly.

"Oh?" He shot her a sideways look. "Not in a good way, if I read you right."

"Maybe too good."

He tossed her a narrow look. "Your parents don't approve?"

"They think you're great. But Hope is still very unhappy, isn't she? She may never accept me."

"Don't say that."

"It's possible."

He squinted. "I don't want to tell her how to feel, so I'm giving her some time to work through her feelings by herself."

"That's so wise, Ben."

"I hope so. She's usually fair. I want to believe she'll revert to that."

"Hope's not the only problem. I told you what happened when I was about to graduate from law school and move to New York on my own."

"You were inexperienced and terrified of launching out on your own. Not sure how that relates to now."

"I lean on you too much, whether you think so or not."

He gave his head a shake. "Not nearly enough, in my opinion."

"You know how important this is to me."

"I'm sorry. But what makes you think you aren't standing on your own? You've been through a lot—survived your husband's death, even gone through pregnancy and childbirth without his support. And here you are, making a new life for yourself and your boys. How much more do you need to do?"

"I survived my husband's death, but the possibility of losing someone else—"

"You're not going to lose anybody."

"You don't know that and neither do I. I do know I *have* to learn to take care of myself and my boys to be strong enough to survive no matter what happens. I will *not* be in the weak, devastating place I was after Cam's death. Not ever again."

He reached out and clasped her hand. "Take the time you

need to completely heal. I don't care how long it takes. Don't you think I want what's best for you?"

"I do. It's just that…things have developed so quickly between us, I'm not sure how to slow them down."

He frowned. "We don't see each other every day now that you're living in your own place."

She held on to his hand like a lifeline. "That doesn't mean I don't *want* to see you every day."

He squeezed her hand. "I was afraid I might be the only one who felt that way."

She wanted so badly to step into his arms. But how would that help? Oh, she was so confused.

"Just tell me what I can do to help, and I'll do it."

Leave it to Ben to want to help. "I'm sorry, but you can't help. Nobody can. I need to do this for myself." With heaviness weighing her down, she twisted her hand out of his grasp. "Please, leave me alone." Unable to look at the shock in his eyes, she turned away and ran all the way back to her cottage, Digger close on her heels.

Chapter Fifteen

Alyssa looked at her image in the mirror and groaned. She looked almost as bad as she felt. Not that she was surprised after crying into her pillow half the night and dozing in fits and starts the other half.

Nothing could erase the look on Ben's face when she'd told him to leave her alone. His hurt had registered as deeply inside her as her own. Sighing, she splashed cold water on her face in an attempt to repair the damage.

Going it alone was the only way. She couldn't go on leaning on him or anybody else. Reaching for the towel, she pressed it to her face to absorb the water. And to muffle the sob that suddenly burst from her.

That afternoon, she took a quick break from working with Reclamation Committee members to ready the fellowship room for tomorrow's fund-raiser. She stopped in the restroom to add more concealer to disguise the dark circles under her eyes. Couldn't have everybody asking her what was wrong, could she?

Returning to the fellowship room, she walked past Pastor Nick's office, the rumble of male voices coming through the closed door. Was he talking to the owner of the faded blue car she'd spotted in the parking lot?

The door opened.

She hurried to allow the man to walk out of the office. "Zebadiah?"

Zebadiah Krentz, spiffed up in his Sunday best, stepped into the hall. "Hello there, missy."

Her overloaded mind stuttered to function. What was the reclusive old man doing here?

Pastor Nick stood in the doorway.

"Don't look so surprised," Zebadiah said. "You're the reason I'm here."

She had no idea what he was talking about. "Excuse me?"

"You been stopping with your boys and that nice boy-friend of yours…bringing all that sunshine with you…even sent Joseph over with Thanksgiving turkey yesterday, didn't you?"

Her mind stopped on "boyfriend." She did her best to catch up. "I told you I'd send my father over with turkey dinner for you. Why didn't you let him in?"

"Habit, I suppose. Told you I never liked people much."

"But you said you wanted to see him."

"Why didn't you come with him?"

"I was busy. And you said you wanted to see my father."

"Well, I changed my mind."

"Why?"

"Too much water under the bridge since I knew him, that's all."

"Hmm. I just found out you bought Gram's cottage and let her pay the money back over the years. Were you worried my father would want to talk to you about that?"

He narrowed his eyes. "Can't say as I was worried."

"But you didn't want to talk about it."

"Still don't. That was between your grandmother and me."

"Thank you for making it possible for her to live her life the way she wanted to."

"Selfish on my part. I looked forward to her summers at Rainbow Lake as much as she did."

"She left the cottage to me."

"She told me."

Alyssa smiled. "Well, my father's staying with me, in case you still want to see him."

"You come with him next time." He looked back at Pastor Nick, a smile flashing deep in his beard. "Isn't she something? A lot like her gramma Emma."

Tears stung Alyssa's eyes. True or not, he couldn't give her a higher compliment.

Pastor Nick smiled his best pastor smile.

"Can't forget my coat." Zebadiah shuffled toward the coatrack. "It's cold out there."

"Can you come in for a minute, Alyssa?" Pastor Nick asked.

Gathering what few wits she could, she stepped into his office.

"That was a nice surprise." Pastor Nick quickly put away communion things from his desk that he'd undoubtedly been using for Zebadiah. "Thank you for your compassion and concern for Zebadiah. I couldn't ask for better results."

"I certainly don't deserve any credit. He and his wife were good friends to my gram and gramps, which makes Zebadiah pretty special to me. Besides, I like him. So does Joey."

He studied her for a moment. "You are already becoming such a vibrant part of our church community. I'm happy you've been attending Sunday services. Are you considering becoming a member here?"

She was surprised by his question, but she liked the idea. "What would I need to do?"

"Meet with me when you have time, and we'll talk about it."

"I will."

"By the way…" The pastor's mouth played with a smile. "'Boyfriend'? Did he mean Ben?"

A flush crept up her neck. "Ben went with me to look at Zebadiah's worn-out generator. Apparently, Zebadiah drew the wrong conclusion."

"Or the right one."

She shook her head, the flush heating her face. She didn't know what to say. Only that she wasn't about to try to explain her situation with Ben to Pastor Nick. "Lots to do." With that, she turned and fled his office.

That evening Coop worked on his computer at the kitchen island, struggling to outline a rough draft of the article he needed to write about the fund-raiser. He could fill in the details when it was over.

But he couldn't focus. Couldn't get his mind off Alyssa. He wanted to go over there and insist she listen to reason. Did she see what they could have together? Understand what she was throwing away?

He still heard the plea in her voice. *Please, leave me alone.* He shook his head. A lot of good going over there would do. He stared unseeingly at the computer screen, trying to wrap his mind around a loss he couldn't accept.

Hope wandered into the kitchen, looking a little lost herself. Without a word, she walked over and draped her arm around his neck like she used to.

He turned on his stool and put his arms around her.

She hugged him back.

What was going on with her? "Love you, kiddo."

"Me, too, you." When she withdrew, she looked at him as if she wanted to say something, then walked away instead. "I'm going to toast a bagel. Want one?"

She sounded more like herself than she had in days. "Sure. Thanks."

She popped bagel halves into the toaster, then planted herself directly across the island from him. "I'm sorry for my bad attitude."

"Apology accepted." He blew out a breath of relief, but she knew it would take more than an apology to him to get her off the hook. She needed to apologize to Alyssa. He couldn't back down on that.

She stared at the countertop. "I'm sorry I was rude to Alyssa. I mean, you aren't rude to my friends, and I shouldn't be rude to yours."

He shut his eyes against her approval of Alyssa as his "friend." She was so much more than that.

"I don't want to lose you, Dad."

He met her eyes. "That's never going to happen. You're my daughter. We're in this together."

"I guess I forgot that for a while when it wasn't just you and me anymore."

He rubbed his forehead. "It will always be you and me, Hope. That will never change. Don't you know that?"

She gave him a skeptical look. "If you and Alyssa start seeing each other, things will change. You might even get married, right?"

"That's not going to happen."

"Because of me." She frowned. "I want you to be happy, Dad. Even I can see she makes you happy. You were right. She has been trying to be my friend. I acted mean, and I'm sorry."

"I'm glad you figured that out."

"Me, too. Thanks for not crowding me."

The toaster popped up. They ignored it.

"You need to tell Alyssa. But just so you know, she and I won't be seeing each other." His words sounded as dead as he felt inside.

Hope squinted at him as if she didn't understand. "But I'll do my best to be okay about you dating her, Dad. Honest."

"I appreciate that. But Alyssa doesn't want to see me."

"She kissed you. Was that a mistake?"

"No, but she's not ready to go out with anybody. Her husband died only a year ago, and she needs space."

"It's because of me. I know it is." She shook her head. "Who'd want a brat like me in the family?"

"Not true. Alyssa thinks you're terrific. She'll be glad you're not upset anymore. But she and I will not be dating." Even as he laid out the truth for his daughter, he couldn't accept it. How could he? Now that he'd finally found the woman he'd been looking for his entire life, how could he learn to live without her?

"I'm gonna go over and apologize to Alyssa while I have my nerve up, okay?"

"Good idea. Do you want me to go with you and wait on the porch?"

She shook her head. "I'm good." She hurried to the laundry room to get her coat.

A couple minutes later, he heard the door close behind her. His little girl was growing up whether he was ready or not, so he'd better get used to it. If it didn't kill him, she'd undoubtedly keep on enlightening him the way she'd done since the day she was born. *Please help us to always stay open to one another, no matter what we're going through.*

As for Alyssa? He was powerless in that situation. He couldn't do a thing to help the woman he loved. *I think I get it, Lord. If I love her, and we both know I do, then I have to back off and respect her decisions. No matter what her decisions are. No matter how hard they might be to accept. I can't make them for her. Please give me the strength I need to do that.*

Please help me remember: not my will, but Yours.

* * *

"Thanks for the trial run, Harold. I won't be long." Very early Saturday morning, Alyssa climbed down from the sleigh, the jingle of sleigh bells punctuating the horses' every move. Trying to brace herself for seeing Ben, she strode under the Christmas-festooned trellis and up the freshly swept brick path toward the Stefano Victorian, majestic and proud in its setting of snow-outlined, towering trees.

She climbed the steps, admiring the tastefully decorated porch and gorgeous swag drawing her eye to the richly paneled front door. Maggie was a genius decorator.

Tony pulled the door wide-open, a string quartet arrangement of "Silent Night" greeting her. "Are you sufficiently impressed?"

"The Victorian looks like a Christmas card. I love your choice of music, too. We have choral Christmas carols playing in the fellowship room. Totally different atmosphere over there. When did you finish decorating outside?"

"About a half hour ago. *Nonna* and Maggie are touching up in the kitchen, and Coop and I are spreading runners on the wood floors."

Was Ben listening to them? Would he at least say hello? Hope's sweet, heartfelt apology last night had touched her deeply. She was so glad Ben and his daughter were in sync again. "It smells divine in here. Cinnamon and bayberry and Fraser. Can't beat that combination. The tree is perfect in that spot, isn't it?" Doing her best to drown out thoughts of Ben with chatter, she smiled at the cats, one black, one white, snuggled up together on the tree skirt under the tree.

Tony chuckled. "Snowball and Vader have made themselves at home."

"You guys did a great job over here."

"Look around, see if we're missing anything. I'd better get back to those runners." He strode away.

She longed to see Ben, even if it would be awkward. But he obviously did not want to see her, and who could blame him? Heart heavy, she wanted to sink to the floor in a frenzy of tears. *Very grown-up, Alyssa.*

She didn't feel grown-up. She felt miserable and overwhelmed, and she missed Ben so much she didn't know what to do. She felt like giving up the whole idea of trying to be an adult. It was just too hard.

But people were counting on her. She needed to pull herself together and get back to the fellowship room.

By late afternoon, people were still arriving to take part in the fund-raiser. The scents of popcorn and hot dogs and sloppy joes rode the air in the fellowship room. The Reclamation Committee was elated by the turnout, even if they were dead on their feet.

The din of people talking and laughing drowned out Christmas music playing in the background. Alyssa walked over to the control board in the corner of the huge room and turned up the volume.

Glancing around for anything that might need attention at the moment, Alyssa focused on Lou's striking quilt displayed on the wall above the bidding table. She loved it more every time she saw it.

"Mommy!" Joey ran up and flung his arms around her legs.

She caressed his cheek. "Hi, honey."

"Grandma and Grandpa and Robbie and me went on the sleigh ride and Mr. Harold let me sit by him again. It was sweet."

"Sweet?" No doubt, that word came straight from Hope.

"Great job." Her father's voice boomed over the din before she saw him making his way through the crowd carrying Robbie in his carrier. "Your mother's going to be wanting a Victorian, I'm afraid. It's magnificent."

Alyssa stroked her sleeping baby because she needed to.

Her mother peeked over one of Maggie's beautiful Christmas centerpieces. "Isn't this extraordinary?" she asked excitedly. "I'd like to transport Maggie to Washington. We need her talent."

"I'm surprised Daddy didn't offer her a job," Alyssa teased.

"Who says I didn't?" her father shot back. "Lot more people here than I expected. Where did they all come from?"

"From all over the state," Alyssa said. "Some have relatives who live in the area, but many saw Ben's advertisements in their local papers."

"That young man's on the ball, no doubt about it. Did he tell you I offered to put in a good word for him with the *Post?* Turned me down flat."

"I'm not surprised."

Daddy shook his head as if he couldn't understand. "Well, I must commend you on the way you're pulling yourself together and making a place for yourself here, Lissa. Of course, I'd prefer you did it in Washington, but you must follow your own path."

She brushed away tears pooling in her eyes. Would she ever have herself together without Ben in her life? "Thanks, Daddy."

He waved away her thanks. "Joey, you ready for a hot dog?"

Gravy, hot dogs…no wonder her father's cholesterol was high. "Mother, I know Daddy loves baked goods, so you might just as well get the good stuff with no preservatives. There's an unbelievable selection, but it's going fast."

"Thanks, dear."

"Look, Grandpa. Here's Dolly. Mr. Max maked horses and pigs, too. And…Digger!" He squealed. "Grandpa, Grandma, you have to see Digger."

Chuckling, her father hurried to his grandson's side, no doubt to raise several bids on Max's toy animals.

"This is the quilt you want for your bedroom, isn't it? It's lovely, dear." Mother checked the bid list. "Very reasonable when you consider it really is a piece of art. I'll bid on it for you."

Obviously, Mother's budget left room for more pieces of art than Alyssa's did, but... "Please don't, Mother. Don't let Daddy buy it for me either. It's something I really want to buy for myself."

"Oh, Alyssa. You and that grandmother of yours."

"Please, Mother."

"Oh, all right. I'll steer your father entirely away from it."

"Thank you."

"Alyssa," Max paged from the food concession.

"Have fun." With a wave to her family, Alyssa made her way through the crowd to find out what Max needed, then hustled off to get more change from the little safe in her office. She decided to escape into the sanctuary for a few minutes of calm.

She made her way up the aisle, knelt at the communion rail and looked up at the cross with a heavy heart as Ben's words drifted through her mind. *My dad told me to lay my weakness at Jesus's feet.*

"I give you my weakness, Lord."

With a few minutes of quiet peace calming her, she thought of Cam, surprisingly without the dread and nausea she'd associated with his death. When was the last time she'd experienced those things? Now, she felt only calm and acceptance. "Thank You."

But there was no calm, no acceptance when she thought about Ben and Hope. Only emptiness. Defeated and weary, she left the sanctuary, retrieved the bank bag of change she needed from her office and hurried back to the fellowship room, determined to make it through the rest of the day the best way she could.

As she walked into the giant room teeming with scents and noise and excited chatter, joy rang in children's voices. Children like Joey, exclaiming over the sleigh ride and Max's wooden toys and Lou's doll clothes.

She heard gratitude from adults inspired by the majestic Victorian and Maggie's exquisite Christmas decorations. People like her parents. She heard appreciation for the long hours of work invested in quilting and sewing and baking delicious food for others to enjoy.

Her parents and children sat eating popcorn at one of the tables. She spotted Pastor Nick, surrounded by several members of the Reclamation Committee who had given all these gifts to others. They had welcomed her into their fold as if she was one of them. They'd not only been her keeper, but they'd also allowed her to be theirs. Where had she ever before found people like these?

Never.

Her gaze homed in on Ben and Hope, the quilt she loved framing them like a backdrop. He met her gaze, his kind eyes filled with caring and hurt.

Her throat closed. She loved him. And his daughter. Then why was she pushing them away?

She'd moved here to gain strength to make it on her own like her gram. But Gram hadn't made it without accepting help, had she? Zebadiah had helped her keep the cottage, so she could continue to live the life she loved.

And Gram hadn't pushed love away either. Hadn't Ben said everybody loved her?

I've had it wrong, haven't I, Lord? Standing on my own doesn't require isolation. That's why You gave me Zebadiah and a community to care about. That's why You gave me Ben and Hope to love.

Please give me the faith and courage to give them the love they deserve.

Looking around at the happy, boisterous crowd, she wanted to embrace them all and tell them she heard God in their voices.

But that wouldn't make her heart sing, would it? Only the love of one very special man could do that.

Chapter Sixteen

Coop lost track of Alyssa in the crowd. She looked tired, but obviously excited about the turnout. People milled around him, happy with the experience they were having. Judging from the lines of people who'd filed through the Victorian all day, the fund-raiser was a bigger success than the Reclamation Committee ever imagined it could be. Thanks to their hard work…and especially to Alyssa's talent and expertise in putting it together and making sure it flowed seamlessly.

Now they'd have the money they needed to buy materials, so Tony and his crew could get to work. Personally, he'd be relieved to get through this day. And the next, and the next. And as many days as it would take to stop missing Alyssa. She'd leave a hole in his life he'd never be able to fill.

When he heard her talking to Tony at the Victorian this morning, she'd sounded so sad. So distant.

He missed her vibrancy and laughter. He missed her holding her baby in her arms and smiling at Joey. He missed her teaching Hope to cook and trying to heal his abandoned little girl's heart. He missed her in his arms, missed the joy and wonder in her eyes.

Sure, she'd live next door. He'd still see her and her little guys sometimes, which would be both a blessing and a curse. And he was still going to buy her the quilt she loved. He wanted her to enjoy it in her mango-punch bedroom.

He glanced at his watch. Bidding would close in two minutes. That was why he was standing guard to make sure he'd have the final bid. He moved to the quilt to look at the list. A name he didn't recognize topped his last bid. He picked up the pen.

"Are you bidding on the quilt?"

His entire system lit up. He'd know that soft, melodic voice anywhere, anytime. He turned to face her.

She eyed the pen in his hand. "I'd like to make the final bid."

He swallowed, ready to protest. But apparently she needed to do this for herself. He relinquished the pen.

Looking a little surprised when she saw the amount she needed to top, she did it quickly and signed her name just as Lou announced the end of the silent auction.

"Congratulations," he said. "It's a beautiful quilt."

"I love you," she said.

Her words took a couple of seconds to register. Another second or two for him to understand them. He didn't know what to think, only knew this was the most important moment in his life. "I love you."

She took a breath. Nibbled her lip as if she was unsure what to say now that they'd both voiced their feelings.

Clasping his hands together to discourage his desire to touch her, he realized he was trembling. From relief? From excitement? From sheer restraint when he wanted to haul her into his arms and never let her go?

"I love Hope, too, you know?"

He nodded. "I know."

"You are the most loving and giving man I've ever known. I want to love like you do."

He frowned, hesitant to believe her words could possibly be promising what he hoped.

She held his gaze as if waiting for him to say something.

His heart thudded hard enough to steal his breath. "I'm so in love with you. I don't know how to live without you. You're perfect exactly the way you are. I want to be perfect for you, too."

"You already are." She reached out and laid her hand along his jaw.

"I can be patient," he whispered, belying the energy her touch spurred. "I promise to give you whatever you need if you tell me what that is. If it's time, you have it. If it's space, you have it. For however long it takes. I'm not going anywhere."

"Maybe we can date?"

He grinned. "Absolutely."

"Sounds like we have a deal, then." She broke into a brilliant smile.

Her smile? He'd always understood that. Needing her in his arms as much as he needed his next breath, he folded her close and kissed her.

Epilogue

More than a year later, Mozart's *Eine kleine Nachtmusik* Romanze swelled in the beautiful church in Noah's Crossing. Stately Frasers Alyssa and Hope had helped decorate with handmade Christian symbols guarded the altar and filled the air with Christmas.

Goose bumps danced over Alyssa's skin. She was so excited to marry Ben. Thankfully, her nerves had taken the day off. Which bothered her a little. If she'd ever had a reason to be nervous, it was probably now because wise or not, she'd included the whole family in the wedding.

She calmly waited for Hope to take a few steps down the aisle with Robbie in her arms. Joey followed. Then Mother on one arm and her father on the other, Alyssa began the most significant walk she'd ever take.

After a remarkable year of healing and growth, their little family had hit a balance of sharing and loving and laughing together that seemed to work for all of them. She smiled. Of course, she'd fallen more in love with Ben than ever. And marrying him in the church they both loved, surrounded with family and friends was perfect.

Their youngest guest? One-year-old Salvatore Anthony Stefano, Tony and Maggie's handsome baby boy in the arms of his big sister, Christa. Oldest guest? Zebadiah Krentz, all decked out in a brand-new suit Ben had helped him find in Eau Claire. Zebadiah had embraced Ben as the grandson he never had. Alyssa couldn't be happier for them both. And Ben's parents had even flown in from Vietnam for the wedding. They were amazing.

The chancel was beautifully decorated with Maggie's poinsettias everywhere. Raising her eyes to the awe-inspiring wood cross over the altar, Alyssa prayed a silent prayer of thanks with a humble request for wisdom and strength to be the wife and mother Ben and their new family deserved. The prayer she prayed every single day.

And then she met Ben's beautiful eyes filled with tears of happiness. She had no tears today. Only smiles for the most loving, incredible man on earth.

"Hi, Ben," Joey said loud and clear.

A chuckle swelled through the church.

"Hi, buddy." Face filled with love, Ben pointed to the spot near Hope and Robbie where Joey had been told to stand.

"Hi." Not one to miss out on the action, Robbie gave Ben and Joey his modified wave.

Alyssa smiled at her sons without a nerve in sight.

Joey confidently moved to his spot.

Ben walked to meet her, his handsome face sporting the smile that always stole her breath.

Her father kissed her cheek; her mother the other. They took turns hugging Ben, then stepped back to allow him to clasp her arm.

Smiling into each other's eyes, she and Ben took a step up and turned to a beaming Pastor Nick. The service was a happy blur. Good thing there would be a video she could savor later. Bubbling with joy, she couldn't wait to respond to the pastor's big question.

Finally, he asked it. "Do you, Alyssa, take Ben Cooper as your husband, to have and to hold until death do you part?"

"We do," Joey piped up.

"Yes, we do," Alyssa confirmed.

"Do you, Ben, take Alyssa Bradley Douglas as your wife, to have and to hold until death do you part?"

"We do," Hope announced.

"We do," Ben repeated.

"Then I pronounce you husband and wife and family. Ben, you may kiss your bride."

So he did.

His kiss spoke of the soul-deep intimacy between two people who love each other. With his encouraging support and God's presence empowering her, she could face the future with confidence and faith.

She believed God had brought their little blended family together to share lives filled with joy and wonder. And she couldn't wait to see what He had planned for them.

Because with God, all things really were possible.

* * * * *

Dear Reader,

Alyssa Douglas has come to a fork in the road since her husband's death a year ago. No longer willing to depend on others to help her raise her two young boys, she is determined to be the mother her children deserve. And she believes the only way to become the strong, self-sufficient woman buried deep inside is to overcome her past weakness and dependence and learn to stand on her own.

Easier said than done. Especially after the daddy next door rescues her and her little boys from a fire. Seems God has a lot more surprises in store for Alyssa and Ben than either could ever imagine. But doesn't He always? All we have to do is to be open to them.

I would love to hear your thoughts and feelings about *Daddy Next Door*. You can write to me at Love Inspired Books, 233 Broadway, Suite 1001, New York, NY 10279, email me at carol@carolvoss.com or visit me on the web at www.carolvoss.com.

Grace always,

Carol Voss

Questions for Discussion

1. The young, pregnant mother of a three-year-old, Alyssa was overwhelmed by her husband's sudden death and unable to take care of her son. Have you ever been in a situation that demanded more from you than you had to give? Explain. What did you do?

2. Alyssa is very grateful for people who helped her through her ordeal. But now she feels she must get away from their help to heal completely. Can you understand her feelings? Have you ever felt this way? How did you deal with it?

3. Alyssa started a chimney fire because of nests or food stashed in the chimney by small animals. Would you make the same mistake? Why or why not?

4. What does Alyssa do with her parents' checks? What would you do with them?

5. What traits do you think make Ben Cooper irresistible to Alyssa? Why is he exactly the man to test her resolve to stand on her own? Does Alyssa have traits that make her his perfect match?

6. Can you understand why Hope will not accept Alyssa? Why is she worried about her dad? Is there anything Alyssa could have done to help the girl? Could Ben have done more to help his daughter?

7. Why do you think Joey was immediately comfortable with Ben? Which interactions between the man and boy paved the way?

8. Who is Ben's mentor? Why? How has his mentor influenced him? Who is Alyssa's mentor? Why? How has her mentor shaped her?

9. Alyssa and her parents have a complicated relationship. Can you understand her parents' concern for their daughter and their grandsons? Can you understand Alyssa's need to become her own person?

10. Did Ben go above and beyond the norm when he adopted Hope? Have you ever known somebody who amazed you with his or her capacity to love? Did this person have a close relationship with God? Are you one of those people?

11. Alyssa dearly loves Joey, but she can't help blaming herself for disappointing her parents, her boyfriend and herself with an unplanned pregnancy. Have you ever had mixed feelings surrounding a choice you made when you were young and inexperienced? Do you understand why you made the choice you did? Are you cautious about making choices as a result?

12. Do you think Ben's mother leaving when he was eight has had a bearing on his avoidance of a serious relationship with a woman? What reason does he give for it?

13. Do you understand why Alyssa finds helping others so rewarding? What do you think it represents to her?

14. Alyssa feels that having a purpose will help her cope with the anniversary of her husband's death. Have you ever faced a difficult anniversary? How did you cope with it?

15. "Inasmuch as ye have done it unto the least of these my brethren, ye have done it unto me." ~Matthew 25:40, King James Version. Have you ever found it difficult to live by these words? Why or why not?

THE BOSS'S BRIDE
The Heart of Main Street
Brenda Minton
Gracie Wilson ran from her wedding and the man who broke her heart...straight into the arms of the man who might change her life.

A FATHER'S PROMISE
Hearts of Hartley Creek
Carolyne Aarsen
When the child she gave up for adoption shows up in town with her adoptive father, Renee must overcome her past to find true love.

NORTH COUNTRY HERO
Northern Lights
Lois Richer
It takes the tender heart of Sara Kane and her teen program to make a wounded former soldier see that home is where he belongs.

FALLING FOR THE LAWMAN
Kirkwood Lake
Ruth Logan Herne
Opposites attract when a beautiful dairy farmer who's vowed never to date a cop falls for the handsome state trooper who lives next door.

A CANYON SPRINGS COURTSHIP
Glynna Kaye
When a journalist arrives in town, will her former sweetheart resist her charms or find a second chance for love?

THE DOCTOR'S FAMILY REUNION
Mindy Obenhaus
After ten years away, Dr. Trent Lockridge hadn't counted on running into Blakely, the girl he should have married. Or the shock of finding out he has a son.

REQUEST YOUR FREE BOOKS!

2 FREE INSPIRATIONAL NOVELS

PLUS 2
FREE
MYSTERY GIFTS

Love Inspired

SPECIAL EXCERPT FROM

Love Inspired

Gracie Wilson is about to become the most famous runaway bride in Bygones, Kansas. Can she find true happiness? Read on for a preview of
THE BOSS'S BRIDE *by Brenda Minton.*
Available September 2013.

Gracie Wilson stood in the center of a Sunday school classroom at the Bygones Community Church. Her friend Janie Lawson adjusted Gracie's veil and again wiped at tears.

"You look beautiful."

"Do I?" Gracie glanced in the full-length mirror that hung on the door of the supply cabinet and suppressed a shudder. The dress was hideous and she hadn't picked it.

"You look beautiful. And you look miserable. It's your wedding day—you should be smiling."

Gracie smiled but she knew it was a poor attempt at best.

"Gracie, what's wrong?"

"Nothing. I'm good." She leaned her cheek against Janie's hand on her shoulder. "Other than the fact that you've moved one hundred miles away and I never get to see you."

What else could she say? Everyone in Bygones, Kansas, thought she'd landed the catch of the century. Trent Morgan was handsome, charming and came from money. She should be thrilled to be marrying him. Six months ago she had been thrilled. But then she'd started to notice little signs. She should have put the wedding on hold the moment she noticed those signs. And when she knew for certain, she should have put a stop to the entire thing. But she hadn't.

"Do you care if I have a few minutes alone?"

"Of course not." Janie gave her another hug. "But not too long. Your dad is outside and when I came in to check on you the seats were filling up out there."

"I just need a minute to catch my breath."

Janie smiled back at her and then the door to the classroom closed. And for the first time in days, Gracie was alone. She looked around the room with the bright yellow walls and posters from Sunday school curriculum. She stopped at the poster of David and Goliath. Her favorite. She'd love to have that kind of faith, the kind that knocked down giants.

"You almost ready, Gracie?" her dad called through the door.

"Almost."

She opened the window, just to let in fresh air. She leaned out, breathing the hint of autumn, enjoying the breeze on her face. She looked across the grassy lawn and saw…

FREEDOM.

To see if Gracie finds her happily-ever-after, pick up
THE BOSS'S BRIDE
wherever Love Inspired books are sold.

LIEXP0813

A FATHER'S PROMISE
by
CAROLYNE AARSEN

When the child she gave up for adoption shows up in
town with her adoptive father, Renee must overcome
her guilt to find true love.

*Available September 2013
wherever Love Inspired books are sold.*